I0547652

# DEAD RINGER

an Al Pennyback mystery

# CHARLES RAY

## North Potomac, MD

This book is a work of fiction. Names, descriptions, places, and incidents are products of the author's imagination, or are used fictionally. Any resemblance to actual events or persons, living or dead, is purely coincidental.

The reproduction or distribution, by any means, including electronic distribution, is expressly prohibited without the written consent of the copyright holder, except for fair use quotes in connection with reviews.

For information about this and other works of this author, contact the author at charlesray.author@yahoo.com.

Cover art and design by the author.

Printed in the United States of America.

Copyright © 2016 Charles Ray

All rights reserved.

ISBN: 0692611509
ISBN-13: 978-0692611500

# Dedication

To those law enforcement officers who believe in their motto, 'To Protect and Serve,' and to the victims of bullies and abusers worldwide.

.

# ONE

It was hump day.

Wednesday, the day of the week when the government drones in Washington, DC are sitting at their desks looking at their inboxes and thinking of the upcoming weekend rather than doing the work your tax dollar is paying them to do. On Wednesday, November 20, 2002, yours truly, while not a government drone, was doing precisely that. I am a private investigator. The name's Al Pennyback, founder and partner in A.E. Pennyback, Confidential Enquiries. The 'A.E.' stands for Albert Einstein, courtesy of a mother who had a thing for the German scientist, and hopes that her only son would grow up to be one; not a German, but a scientist, but I disappointed her by joining the army right out of high school, and thanks to a junior high school growth spurt and the ability to use my fists effectively, no one, and I do mean no one, calls me anything other than Al, or Mr. Pennyback.

I sat in the scuffed leather executive chair I'd acquired from an auction of surplus government property nearly ten years ago, behind the large mahogany executive desk, acquired in the same auction. We were between cases, Heather and I. The law firm of Holcombe, Stein and Chang, where my old army buddy, Quincy Chang was a senior partner, and the company that had me on a ten thousand dollars a month retainer to do odd investigative jobs, thanks to his intervention, hadn't sent us a case in two weeks—probably because everyone was getting ready for Thanksgiving and the post-Thanksgiving Christmas shopping, and nothing had come in over the transom. During times like this, I either sat at my desk with the chair turned to face the window and gazed out toward the Washington Ship Channel, a tiny sliver of blue through the profusion of maple and oak trees set among the shiny condos that hovered over our building like mountains, or I played chess on the new laptop computer Heather had insisted I buy; her effort to bring me into the twenty-first century, she said. The weather had been cold, so most of the leaves had fallen, leaving just a few brown and orange holdovers clinging precariously to gray limbs. This gave me a better view of the channel, and the spires of sailboat masts, and even a glimpse of the Potomac just beyond, and an occasional look at planes landing at National Airport.

I'd begun the morning playing chess against the computer, but after getting mated the fifth time, I'd given it up, and just sat there, the back of my chair against the desk, looking at the trees, condos, and masts. Not much else to see. My office is pretty spartan. Other than my desk and chair, there was a straight-back wooden chair for visitors, set at the left side of my desk, a three-shelf bookcase with PI manuals, phone books, and books of maps, that I hardly ever used, a couple of reproduction of hunting scenes that Heather had bought in a book store somewhere and framed to give the office a look of sophistication or something, and a framed and autographed color photo of me in my uniform with my new colonel's leaves on the epaulets standing next to General Colin Powell when he was Chairman of the Joint Chiefs of Staff. Along with several other newly-promoted bird colonels, I'd been given the chance to have my photo taken with the chief, and he'd nicely signed it, **Congratulations, Al, warmly, Colin Powell**. It was the only memento of my military service I displayed, and I had it on the wall near the door so I could see it from behind my desk.

The photo and prints helped to take my mind off the fact that the walls were in need of a coat of paint. The institutional green color had faded to almost white, and was beginning to crack in places.

The PI firm, and I use that term generously

since we are a two-person outfit—just me and my one time assistant, now partner, Heather Bunche—is housed in a down-at-the-heels building just off Fourth Street in the Southwest area of the District, a few blocks south of the Waterfront Metro Station. We're on the second floor of a building that looks a lot like those motels on the side of the back roads in some southern states, with names like Bide-a-While and Dew Drop Inn. The ongoing gentrification of the area, with gleaming high-rise condos sprouting up like weeds in a vacant lot, just adds to the seediness of our appearance.

But, the rent's cheap and while we do have roaches, the landlord's pretty good about keeping the rats out—at, least the four-legged kind. The two-legged variety, *rodentia bipedia*, if that's even a word, had an annoying way of finding their way to us. When you're in the PI business, though, it comes with the territory.

I'd lost count of the number of planes I'd watched skimming in over the tips of the sailboat masts, so I decided to start over. By the time I got to five, I was already bored, and just about to turn around and let the computer humiliate me for a few more games, when Heather breezed into my office. Well, not exactly breezed; she had a look on her face that was somewhere between confused and pissed off.

"What's up, honeybunch?" I asked, using the pet name that she hated, but would let me, and only me, get away with.

"There's a guy outside who says he needs a

private dick, and I'm not kidding, that's exactly what he said," she said. "And, he says he'll only talk to you."

"Did you tell him that you are also a licensed private investigator?"

She put a hand on her hip and struck a pose, with her hip angled out to the side and a 'what the hell do you think' look on her face.

"Okay," I said. "So, you told him. What'd he say to that?"

"He said, nothing personal little lady." Her expression changed to 'if you don't talk to this guy I'm gonna smack him in the face.' "But, I need to talk to Al Pennyback. He was personally recommended."

"By who?"

"It's by whom," she said. "And, he wouldn't say."

"Well, shit, if he won't tell you *who* referred to him, maybe you should tell him to take a hike."

She rolled her eyes. Lately I'd taken to deliberately using bad grammar just to rile her. It was partly in retaliation for her bugging me about writing my memoirs—I mean, really, who the hell would want to read about a recycled army officer who runs around pretending to be a PI—but, partly because the expressions on her face when I split infinitives or some other mindless grammar rule like that were priceless.

"I told him that," she said. "A bit less direct, and more polite than that, but he said it was extremely important, and he really emphasized extremely."

I sat there for a few seconds, looking up at the ceiling. I noticed a few new cracks, and a flap of paint hanging near the light fixture.

She folded her arms under her ample chest and stood there tapping her feet.

"Well, are you going to talk to him or not?" she finally asked.

"Hell, I might as well," I said. "Not like I've got anything else to do."

It was too early for lunch, and I didn't really want to play any more chess.

Heather disappeared back into the outer office, which we used to call reception, but now that she's a partner we've taken to calling it the outer office. Might as well call it the main office, since, except for the few case notes I keep in steno pads which I keep in my desk drawers, everything we have that means anything is kept there.

She was back in my doorway a few seconds later and just barely had time to step aside when a force of nature blew in past her.

That is the only way I can describe Jackson Meredith—he was giving me his name before he'd covered half the distance to my desk, and sitting in the guest chair without even waiting for me to ask him to take a seat.

"I'm Jackson Meredith," he said in a booming voice like a high school football coach. "And, I need you to find my wife."

# TWO

Jackson Meredith was a big man. Big head, broad shoulders, big gut, big shoes, and a big voice. He stood about half an inch shorter than my six feet, but had at least forty pounds on my two-twenty. He wore a fifteen hundred dollar blue suit, the buttons of the jacket almost popping from the effort of keeping his gut in check, black Prada wingtips, and smelled as if he'd slept under the men's cologne counter at Macy's. Over his left arm, he casually carried a beige cashmere coat that probably cost more than we paid each month for rent. When he sat down and leaned forward to offer his meaty hand for a shake, I could smell the odor of stale tobacco on his breath—probably smuggled Cuban cigars. That's the impression he gave. A rich man with more money than sense, and bad personal hygiene.

"Look, Mr. Meredith," I said. "We're not in the business of finding mates for people. This is an investigation agency, not a matchmaker."

The way his fat lips curled down, and the blaze of anger in his yellow-brown eyes, I don't think he appreciated my attempt at humor.

"I don't appreciate your attempt at humor," he said. "I'm not looking for *a* wife; I'm looking for *my* wife. She's gone missing."

Oh, so it wasn't a joking matter. Time to get serious.

"We also don't do missing persons," I said. "You should go to the police."

"That won't do any good."

"You mean, she hasn't been missing 72 hours? You're right, they don't like to start investigating until they're sure, but that's just three days, right. You don't think your wife's in any danger, do you?"

He was looking even more frustrated. He clenched his fists that he was holding on his legs, and glared at me. I was willing to bet that he'd have words with whoever recommended me—which remind me not to let him leave without finding out who that was, so I could give them a piece of *my* mind.

"You don't get it, Pennyback." Now, that kind of pissed me off. He was either being deliberately rude, or was so rich he was accustomed to treating everyone else like a subordinate. "There's no use going to the cops because they think Caroline, that's my wife's name, is dead."

*Now* he had my attention. I still didn't like him—just on general principle—but, what he'd just said intrigued me. If the cops thought his wife was dead, why in hell would he want to hire me to find her?

"Why do the cops think your wife's dead?"

A little of the anger in his eyes faded. Nothing like asking a question related to a person's problem to make them think you're interested in that problem. Actually, I was a bit interested. Not enough yet to take him on as a client, I just wanted to know what was going on.

"I'll have to give you a bit of background," he said. "Then, maybe you'll understand why I think the cops are fulla shit."

He then proceeded to tell me a story that left me convinced that *someone* was full of shit—I just wasn't sure who.

Meredith owned a property develop company, building shopping centers and office buildings all over the DC, Maryland, and Virginia area, and even occasionally as far north as Delaware and Pennsylvania. His work required him to do a lot of travel, even abroad from time to time. He and his wife had been married for six years, her first, and his third. He'd been on a business trip—he wouldn't say what kind of business—to Hong Kong until five days previously. Eight days prior, his wife had been killed—reportedly killed, according to him—in an auto accident. Her body had been badly disfigured in the wreck, but her father, Matt Donahue, had identified it, been given custody, and had her immediately cremated.

"Seems pretty cut and dry to me," I said when he'd finished. "What makes you think she's still alive?"

For the first time since entering my office an expression of something other than disdain or anger crossed his face. For the briefest of moments I was sure I saw sadness.

"I just know it," he said in a low voice. "Look, her old man never liked me from the start. Matter of fact, the son of a bitch hates my guts because I got money and he's a broken down old bum living on a pension check."

He paused to wipe at his eyes.

"It just doesn't make sense," he continued. "I mean, it was like he rushed to cremate her. Couldn't even wait for me to get back into the country—didn't even notify me she was dead. I found out by seeing it on a TV in the airport lounge in San Francisco when I was waiting to change planes. The day she was cremated . . . the day the body they say was hers was cremated."

"Whoa," I said. "Her father ID'ed the body? Surely the man knew his own daughter. *That* doesn't make a whole lot of sense."

My brain was zipping along like a luge in the final stretch of the Olympic run. Okay, maybe the father could have—should have—waited for the husband to return before the cremation, but he'd said his wife's father didn't particular like him, so I suppose I could see him doing that out of spite or something. What I couldn't easily get my mind around was the idea that the cops would have released the wrong body to a next of kin. But, he had an answer to that one too.

"You'd of thought so," he said. "And, according to the cop I talked to, the body wasn't that damaged—at least, not the face, so he shouldn't have had a problem. They said he was pretty certain that the body on the slab was Caroline, and since it was a one-car accident, no evidence of alcohol or drugs; but there was some ice on the road, they wrote it off as just a freak accident and turned the remains over to him. When I pitched a fit that *I* was her legal next of kin and they should have waited for me, he said she had a card in her wallet listing her *father* as next of kin and having the power of attorney to make medical decisions, whatever the hell that is. Anyway, the cop just blew me off; saying that blood relatives with that kind of authorization from the deceased are legal and acceptable, so, basically . . . piss off."

"I can see why you're upset, Mr. Meredith, but that still doesn't mean your wife's alive. Did you ask the police for some kind of proof, DNA evidence for example?"

"Yeah, I did, and I was told they didn't do one, since there was no indication of foul play, and since the father ID'ed her, no question about who she was."

That sort of made sense. Contrary to what you see on TV, the cops don't routinely do DNA tests. They take a long time, and they're pretty expensive, so they save them for the real tough cases where crimes are committed. A one-car accident, a freak of nature, probably wouldn't be high on their list of things to spend limited department funds on. Still, he had a point. There was something fishy about the whole thing.

"So, you want me to prove that the body your father-in-law had cremated was not your wife, and that your wife's still alive?"

"Damn right I do," he said. "Will you take the case?"

It went against my better judgment. There has to be a little chemistry between me and a client, and I still didn't like this guy. But, it was a puzzle, and I don't like unsolved puzzles. Besides, five hundred a day plus expenses is not something you wave off. Every dollar in the bank account helps. And, I was bored.

"Okay. See my partner outside about a contract and the retainer, write down your wife's name, social security number, date and place of birth, and anything else that might help identify or locate her."

"When will you get started?"

"I just did," I said.

# THREE

After Meredith signed a contract, wrote a check for a five thousand dollar retainer, and departed, Heather and I huddled at her desk.

"Okay, where do you want me to start on this?" she asked.

Now, that was a good question. Usually, I start a case by focusing on what I'd been hired to do. But, in this case, finding a woman who was supposed to already be dead, but whose body had been cremated, didn't give me a lot of starting points. Or, looked at another way, it gave me nothing really to start with.

"I guess you should start with the auto accident," I said. "Then, do a work up on the victim and her family." I rubbed at my chin. Something was itching, and it wasn't the stubble on my cheek. "And, while you're at it, do a complete background check on Jackson Meredith."

She looked surprised, her pen poised over the steno pad on her desk.

"You have a reason for investigating our client, Al?"

"Let's just say that I think there's more to Mr. Meredith than meets the eye. I like to know who I'm working for. Oh, one other thing; Meredith was cagey when I asked him who referred him to me. See if you can find out who that is."

Heather and I have worked together for over a decade. I'd trust her with my life. She's the closest thing to a sister I've ever had. I was an only child, and so was she; and she's petite and blonde, while I'm over six feet and my skin's the color of caramel, but that's never kept us from getting along and trusting each other. She merely nodded, and made a few notes in that precise, neat handwriting of hers. Heather is a computer genius. She can make a computer do things you wouldn't believe, and I never ask her how she does it. But, unlike a lot of computer geeks who are uncomfortable with pen and paper, she writes like one of those ancient scribes who penned those beautiful manuscripts.

"Okay, boss, you got it," she said. She turned and put those beautifully manicured fingers of hers on her keyboard and started typing.

That was my signal to go back to my office, or anywhere else away from her so she could do her magic.

I looked at my Bulova. It was 11:50. Close enough to lunch, so I got my jacket, went out and hopped into my green Volkswagen. I sat behind the wheel for a few minutes trying to decide where to go, finally settling on my favorite lunch spot, the Officers' Club at Fort McNair, an army base just down the street from us.

The MP at the gate gave my army retiree ID card a little extra scrutiny after stopping me, a legacy of the September 11, 2001 attack. Every military base and government building, and not a few civilian organizations, had become extremely paranoid since terrorists had flown planes into the World Trade Center buildings in New York City and the Pentagon, with more stringent ID checks and vehicle searches—and, don't get me started on the hassle for airline passengers. Thankfully, the young sergeant at the gate must have figured I was righteous, so he let me through without a vehicle search, and, he saluted me as I drove away.

A week before Thanksgiving, with many people already taking holiday leave, except the students at the National War College and other schools on the base, the dining room at the club was only sparsely occupied, so I got quick service. They were serving pre-Thanksgiving fare in honor of the holidays, so I had roast turkey, mashed potatoes, cloverleaf rolls, sweet corn, and cranberry sauce, washed down with unsweetened iced tea.

I was stuffed, so I passed on dessert, which

depressed me, since it was pumpkin pie with whipped cream topping.

Feeling virtuous for skipping dessert, I returned to the office. My virtue was rewarded. During lunch, Heather had come up with a ton of information relating to our case, all of which she'd neatly jotted down in her steno pad, because she knows how I hate trying to read things on a computer screen.

She started with the accident that allegedly claimed Caroline Meredith's life.

In her little Honda Civic, she was returning from Germantown, Maryland, where she'd been visiting her father, a widower. It was, according to the police report, around one in the morning, and there was little traffic on Great Seneca Highway, just north of Gaithersburg, when her car, which the cops estimated was traveling at around 70 mph at the time, hit a patch of ice in the road, skidded, flipped and hit a utility pole. The pole crumpled the front of the vehicle and sent the engine back a foot. The deployment of her airbag kept the steering wheel and column from mutilating her, but the weight of the engine was too much even for the airbag, and she was crushed. A late night trucker came upon the accident shortly afterwards, called for help on his CB, and waited for the police to arrive, but the victim was pronounced dead at the scene by the EMTs who arrived with the police. The police checked the scene carefully, which, thanks to the light traffic, was fairly undisturbed—if you can think of a mangled car undisturbed—and found only her skid marks beginning at the site of a large patch of ice that had formed early in the evening and, because of the light traffic, hadn't been broken up.

They found her purse intact on the seat beside her, and inside it found her emergency contact card and driver's license. They called, Matt Donahue, her father, listed as the emergency contact, and he came immediately to the morgue in Rockville and identified the body. Two days later, after a cursory post-mortem exam, the remains were released to Donahue, and the Montgomery County cops closed the case.

The next batch of information was on the victim herself. Caroline Meredith, nee Donahue, was 36 at the time of her death. The daughter of Matt and Elizabeth Donahue, she'd been born in Germantown, Maryland, had graduated from Germantown High School, and gone on to the University of Maryland in College Park, Maryland. Her degree in English hadn't really qualified her for gainful employment, so she'd taken secretarial courses and gone to work as a receptionist-secretary for her soon-to-be husband's property development company in Northeast DC, not far from the UM campus. The information Heather found indicated that she'd been hired by Noah Whelan, a partner in the firm, WheMer Developers. Not long after starting work, she and the firm's junior partner, Jackson Meredith, developed a relationship, and they married. They lived in a large mansion in DC on, of all places, Lovers Lane, near Dumbarton Oaks Park and Montrose Park. Caroline Donahue was an only child. Her mother, a North Carolinian her father met when he was a Marine stationed at Camp Lejeune, died when she was twelve, and she'd lived with him until she went off to college.

"Not a whole lot there," I said.

"Not a . . . oh, not you didn't say that," she said. "I gulped my lunch to get this stuff." She snapped the pad shut.

"Just kidding." I raised my hands in mock surrender. "Actually, this is great, especially for such a short amount of time."

Shrugging, she said, "Yeah, but all it does is support the police view that Caroline Meredith died as a result of injuries sustained in a terrible, one-car accident. There's nothing here to suggest she's alive. I think her poor husband's just in denial, maybe from the grief of losing her."

That was a possibility, but Jackson Meredith didn't strike me as the delusional type. He struck me as a man firmly grounded in reality and accustomed to getting his way. I didn't want to argue with Heather, though. Sometimes she's right.

"Were you able to get anything on Meredith?" I asked just to change the subject.

She flipped the pad open.

"Not as much as on his wife," she said. "But, I did her and her family first. I need to spend more time on him."

"Well, show me what you have."

She was right, it wasn't much. Jackson Meredith, for a wealthy businessman, didn't appear often in the media. Reportedly from New Jersey, he'd come to the DC area in his twenties, working in construction. About ten years ago, he'd thrown in with Noah Whelan, and the two of them had started WheMer Developers, which originally was just a construction firm, but had since morphed into a broker of big commercial development deals. Back in October, Whelan, the senior partner had taken off for parts unknown, accused of bilking the company out of five million dollars. There was nothing about Meredith's family, education, or military service. But, I reminded myself, Heather had just started looking.

"That's all," she said. "There's more in files somewhere. I just have to keep looking."

"Good. Add one more name to your look-up list—"

"Noah Whelan," she said, interrupting me. "Kind of thought you'd be curious about a missing partner and missing money. It has nothing to do with the case we're hired to work, but I know you and puzzles. Besides, there might be a reward for Whelan's capture."

I hadn't thought about that, but it was a bonus.

"Look into that," I said. "We can always use the extra money. Say, did you get any hint of who referred Meredith to us?"

"Nope, not a clue."

Charles Ray

# FOUR

I left Heather to her research and spent the rest of the afternoon in my office running everything through my mind. No, actually, I spent the afternoon playing chess until 4:30, when I decided to hell with it and went home.

Home's an old farmhouse out off River Road just west of Potomac Village in Montgomery County. I bought it after my wife and son were killed in an auto accident and I could no longer stand to be in the little brick house we'd lived in in Georgetown. It was in an estate sale—the old man who owned it had died, and his sons, who lived on the west coast, didn't want to hang on to it.

The house was in pretty good condition, but I tore out the kitchen and had all new appliances installed. Except for reinforced windows and doors, installed after a couple of goons broke in and kidnapped me, the rest of the house was left as it was when I bought it.

Behind the house is a barn. I use it to store excess junk and as a place to hang my heavy bag which I use for workouts. Behind the barn is a bit of open area and then the forest starts, a lot of birch, pine, oak, and maple, as well as some tress types I don't recognize, growing all the way to the C&O Canal and from there to the Potomac River. I let the grass in back grow wild. It makes good fodder for the herds of deer that graze there year round. The front I keep mowed close. I don't think there are any poison snakes in Maryland, but there's no sense taking chances.

You could drive right past the gravel road to my house. It has heavy bush to either side, and is only wide enough for one car, so unless you knew where to look you'd drive right past it. I'm on the River side of River Road, a bit past the ornate mansions, but not quite yet to the remaining farms. Technically, I'm outside Potomac Village, in one of the county's many unincorporated areas. But, the Post Office in Potomac delivers my mail, so to those not in the know I live in Potomac, Maryland, which is considered something of a ritzy address in the Washington area, where movie stars, former politicians, and other rich people live.

The tires on the Bug, which is what I'd taken to calling my Volkswagen, made a sound like crackling paper as they ran over the gravel surface. Other than that, it was quiet. I like that about where I live. There's not all that much traffic on that part of River Road and the trees between the house and the road blocks what there is. It's great when the weather's nice. Sandra and I can sit on the back porch and watch the stars and listen to the chirping of the crickets without the competition from truck engines, sirens, or any of the other noises that plague city dwellers.

And Sandra was waiting for me. Her car, a new blue Toyota Corolla she'd purchased the previous summer, was parked in its usual place near the front porch. Sandra Winter, a teacher at Carter High School in the District's Southeast, is blonde like Heather, but where Heather is short and petite, Sandra's almost my height, and has muscle and flesh in all the right places and in generous amounts. I met her several years back when I'd been hired to investigate the shooting death of one of her students. A bright kid, with a bright future, he'd been gunned down on the sidewalk a few blocks from his house. The cops had written off as a gang feud, but the kid's grandmother was adamant that her grandson had never been involved with street gangs, and hired me to prove it. At one point in the investigation, I'd suspected Sandra of being involved, and had been stupid enough to tell her so, which earned me a slap that hurt like hell. It turned out that her neighbor, the asshole who had accused her, was involved in an art theft ring, and when the kid accidentally saw him and his henchmen moving some of their stolen look, he'd had the thugs kill him.

Fortunately, I helped nab the bad guy, and made up with Sandra. We've been an item ever since. In fact, she's all but moved from her tidy little house in Takoma Park, and stays at my—our—place full time. We've been dancing around the L word like two junior high school students at their first boy-girl dance, even we both know how we feel about each other. At least, I know how I feel about her, and I sense the feeling is mutual. It's just that both of us were on our own for so long, we're having trouble taking that final step.

That doesn't keep us from having a good relationship, emotional and otherwise.

I parked my car next to hers and let myself in. I could hear sounds from the kitchen, sounded like two people singing. When I walked in, she was standing at the kitchen counter, chopping celery and singing along to an old pop tune being played on the local PBS station. She was so engrossed in her chopping and singing, she didn't seem to be aware of my presence, so I slipped up behind her and slipped my arms around her waist, pressing myself against her well-rounded, well-muscled rump. She squealed and twisted around in my arms.

"Albert Pennyback, don't sneak up on me like that, especially when I have a sharp knife in my hand," she said. She frowned, and then completely undercut her effort to look fierce by planting a nice, wet kiss on my lips.

After a long kiss, which made me want to take her right there on the counter, I pulled back.

"I'm not so sure I'm comfortable kissing a woman who has a deadly weapon in her hand," I said, gesturing at the knife she still held.

She looked down. "Look who's talking," she said. "Feels like you're packing some heavy heat yourself."

We both realized where talk like that was likely to lead, and it looked like she'd put some effort into making dinner, so I wasn't about to spoil it. I pulled away from her—reluctantly.

"What are we having for dinner?" I asked, hoping a conversation about food would ease the tension.

She smiled; one of those come hither smiles that made my insides feel like pudding. She reached up and unbuttoned the top button of my shirt.

"Each other," she said.

Ten minutes later, with the kitchen counter and our clothing in disarray, we decided a before dinner shower was in order. The shower took fifteen minutes because Sandra decided as she was soaping my back that she wanted dessert.

Afterwards, with me in a Nike sweatshirt and jeans, and her in an Adidas sweat suit—I didn't even what she'd been wearing in the kitchen, we sat at the little table in the breakfast nook just off the kitchen and ate the tuna salad with croutons she'd so laboriously prepared. Along with the salad, we had a bottle of The Dreaming Tree California pinot noir that I'd picked up at the beer and wine store in Potomac Village. This was one of the impacts hanging around with Sandra had had on me. I'm not really a wine drinker, and before her, wine to me was red or white, sweet or dry, and that was the extent of my knowledge of fermented grape juice. She, on the other hand, while not a wine snob, knew which wine went with which meat, the difference between pinot noir and cabernet sauvignon, and some of it was beginning to rub off on me.

After dinner, we curled up on the couch with the radio tuned to a PBS station. They were playing Bach, which is as good as anything to curl up to, and with the temperatures outside hovering around 38° F, sitting on the back porch and looking at the stars was a nonstarter.

Sandra sat with her shapely legs curled underneath her body and her head nestled in the crook of my shoulder with a glass of wine in her hand. I'd had two glasses with the salad, which is about my limit, and had switched to Dos Equis. I was drinking straight from the bottle, which I'd stuffed a sliver of lime in for extra flavor. The sound of the wind blowing across the roof shingles and through the nearby trees, like the roar of surf at the beach, competed with Bach's *Keyboard Concerto in D*.

After taking a sip of her wine, and then licking her lips like a cat, she looked up at me.

"So, how was your day?"

I told her about the case. I do that a lot. She's a good listener for one thing, and for another, she sometimes sees something about a case that I missed. When I'd finished, though, she just sat there looking at me with a puzzled frown.

"You are kidding, right?" she asked. "This guy's wife died in an accident, but he wants you to find her because he believes she's still alive?"

"That about sums it up."

"He sounds like a nutcase to me."

"That was my first reaction," I said. "But, the guy's more of a hard case than a nutcase, I mean, other than his insistence that his wife's not dead, he acted rational."

Her eyes narrowed, and her forehead creased into a little 'v' shape between her eyebrows.

"Could something like that even happen?"

"Babe, this is Washington, the town that gave you the McCarthy Hearings and Watergate," I said. "In this town, *anything* can happen."

She sat up and twisted around to stare into my eyes. It was hard to concentrate with those dark blue eyes of hers a few inches from mine.

"Tell me," she said. "How does it happen? How do the police, her father, and the medical examiner's office . . . not to mention the EMTs who went to the scene . . . make something like that happen? I mean, the father . . . he'd know his own daughter. It doesn't make any sense."

"That's not the only strange thing about this

case. Someone referred this guy to me, and he wouldn't tell me who."

In some ways that bothered me even more than the improbability of his wife still being alive. My circle of friends is limited. There's Sandra,—yes, I think of her as a friend first, and a lover second—and, of course, Heather. I've known Quincy Chang for years. He was a young JAG lawyer at Fort Bragg, North Carolina when I worked special ops out of there. Buster Mayweather is a DC Metro Police detective. He escorted two uniform cops from Virginia to my house in Georgetown the night my family was killed, and stayed with me through the trauma of identifying their bodies in the Arlington County morgue. We've been friends ever since. His wife, Alma, is smaller than Heather, but as tough and intimidating as a Special Forces A Team, and she and Sandra are as close as identical twin sisters. Buster and Alma named Sandra and me the god parents of their twins, Albert and Sandra—yeah, named them after us as well. Finally, on my list of people I call friend is Carlton 'Blood' Raine, an octogenarian retired CIA agent—one of the first blacks to serve as a field agent anywhere other than Africa, and a specialist in paramilitary operations, and his girlfriend Elizabeth Sung. I'd met Blood through Quincy when I needed some help dealing with a Chinese gangster who was out to kill me, and met Elizabeth when I rescued her from that same bad guy. When Blood and Elizabeth became an item, she sort of got added to my friend list by default, but she and Sandra hit it off right away, so it worked. That's it; the entire universe of people I call friend, and if any of them had referred Meredith to me . . . well, they would have asked first or at least given me a heads up.

Acquaintances are a different matter. As a PI, you meet a lot of people, some only briefly, and some for extended periods. Depending on the case you're working, that can mean a kind of relationship develops. You get to know each other. It never rises to the level of friendship, but you sort of stay in tenuous touch. It's kind of like having a neighbor that you say hello to, but you never invite over for drinks. I tried running through my mind the people I'd met who might send a case my way, and there was no one I could remember who would travel in the same circles as someone like Meredith

Knowing that wouldn't help me solve the case, but it was an unanswered question, and I hate unanswered questions. Besides, I had a sinking feeling that there was no way I *could* solve this case. If Meredith really thought his wife was alive, he wasn't likely to believe any argument I presented to the contrary. I still wasn't ready to accept that she was alive, because that was a whole other problem.

Sandra's accustomed to my obsession with puzzles, and probably recognized this digression as another one. She ignored my whining and changed the subject.

"You know; you should talk to someone who

understands the legal system and get an idea of how a mistake like this is even possible before you waste too much time looking for a dead woman."

See what I mean? The woman comes at the problem from a completely different direction, and points me in the direction I need to go to keep from running in place.

That night I rewarded her for her contribution to the investigation.

# FIVE

The next morning, I rose early to do my morning run. The back yard was white with the frost coating the grass and clinging to the bare branches of low bushes. It made a crunchy sound under my running shoes like paper bags make when you crush them. My breath came out in billows of white mist as I ran my four miles, two down toward the canal, and two back up. I did twenty minutes kicking and punching the heavy bag in the barn, working up a sweat despite the frigid air, and then sat on a mat in the corner of the barn and meditated for ten minutes.

I meditate every day, sometimes multiple times. Not the contorted position, eyes glazed, chanting stuff you see in the movies. I just sit, or stand, for a few minutes and let every muscle in my body relax. I open my palms with the thumb and second finger touching lightly, relax my eyelids and keep my eyes open, and then just . . . *be* for anywhere from two to twenty minutes. I don't go into a trance or block out the world, and it's not a spiritual thing for me. I open my senses to the world around me, and hear without listening, feel without touching, and see without looking. I become one with the moment. It lowers my blood pressure, relaxes my muscles, and removes tension. It gets me ready to face whatever the day throws at me.

After meditating I went in to shower. Sandra was just swinging out of bed.

"Why didn't you wake me up to exercise with you?" she asked. She stretched and yawned. Her body did amazing things to the tee shirt she slept in.

"I thought you got enough exercise last night," I said. "So, I decided to let you sleep. I'm gonna shower and fix breakfast, so if you want to catch a few more z's, go ahead."

"No, I think I'll go work out a few minutes, and then shower."

She pulled the tee off. Damn, she wasn't wearing anything underneath it, making me want to postpone my shower. But, she quickly slipped on a pair of dingy sweats, socks and running shoes and left. I shrugged and showered.

I was dressed for work, dark brown cotton slacks and a blue wool shirt, and whipping up a skillet of scrambled eggs, when she came in from her run. She wasn't even winded. She paused briefly to kiss me on the tip of the nose, and then ran off to shower and change. I ladled the eggs onto a platter next to four slices of bacon, and then checked the biscuits. They were beginning to brown on top, so I turned off the oven to let them finish and began peeling potatoes and onions. I chopped up the potatoes and onions and put them into a bowl with black paper, garlic powder, a pinch of salt and some cumin. Then, after getting about an eighth of an inch of vegetable oil smoking hot in an iron skillet, I dumped this mixture in and with a wooden spatula stirred it around until the potato chunks were light brown and the onion looked almost burned.

I'd filled two plates with eggs, bacon, biscuit and potatoes by the time Sandra breezed back in, dressed in a beige, body-hugging pant suit. I don't remember high school teachers looking that sexy when I was in school, and I wondered how the boys, with their raging hormones, paid any attention to lessons with her in front of them looking like she'd just stepped off the cover of *Women's Health.* I poured us two cups of freshly brewed Jamaican coffee and two glasses of apple juice and we fell to. Both of us have good appetites, and try to never start the day without a robust breakfast. The difference is that I have to work like hell to keep that breakfast from going to my love handles or jowls, while Sandra seems to just sweat the calories off.

After breakfast, I shooed her out and cleaned up the kitchen. Before starting out, I called Heather to let her know I'd be late, called Buster and asked him to see if he could get the Montgomery County Police to share Caroline Meredith's accident report, promising I'd buy him lunch at Mom's in payment. Finally I called Quincy to let him know I was on my way to his office.

I was starting with Quincy first because I really didn't know where else to start. His firm's clients included a lot of the movers and shakers in the region, so I figured he might know something about Meredith.

Quincy has a corner office in the suite—the entire floor of the building—occupied by Holcombe, Stein and Chang. The building is on K Street, a block north of the White House, on that stretch of K Street known as Lobbyists' Row because of the number of law firms and fulltime lobbyists camping out there. I parked in the basement garage and took the elevator to the lobby, where, after showing my ID to the guard at the desk, I was shown to an elevator that took me to their floor.

When you step out of the elevator, you're surrounded by elegance. Maroon carpet stretches to infinity, silver buckets strategically placed hold palms and other tropical looking plants, and little conversation nooks dominate the front area. The back has a large glass-topped desk behind which sits a trim looking young receptionist who had the build of one of the athletes from Georgetown University's rowing team—which he probably was, actually. I could never remember his name, but he recognized me and waved me down the corridor leading to Quincy's office.

Outside his office, Quincy has one of the most efficient gate keepers in the world. With her blue hair and slightly heavy eye liner, Gertrude Larson doesn't look over sixty, but, Quincy assured me, she's actually sixty-eight. Well past retirement age, but he says she's so good at what she does, he's decided to let her work until *she* decides she's ready to quit. She loves to flirt with me, and I flirt back—always keeping her desk between us just in case.

She spent thirty seconds flirting as usual before stabbing the intercom button to let Quincy know I was there, then made a grab at my butt as I passed her desk a bit too close on the way into his office.

Quincy was seated behind his desk, wearing a pearl shirt with red power tie and red suspenders. His gray suit coat hung on a rack near his left side. The top of the kidney-shaped desk was clear except for a thin laptop, two silver metal trays; one for incoming and one for outgoing documents; and a space-age looking telephone with more buttons than a granny dress. Quincy Chang is third generation Chinese-American. Born and raised in southern California, he went to UCLA law school, and entered the army as a JAG lawyer right after graduating and passing the bar exam. A sharp legal mind, he's never been married, much to the dismay of his traditional-minded Chinese parents, but he's hardly ever without female companionship, another thing that pisses his tiger mother mom off.

"Hey, Al," he said. "What legal problem causes you to cross my threshold this early on a Thursday morning?"

Yeah, he talks like that.

"It's not really a legal problem," I shot back. "I just got a new client yesterday, with a bitch of a case, and I need to run something by you."

"That sounds suspiciously like a legal issue to me."

"Well, okay . . . maybe it is. Let me explain." And, I tried to. I gave him a rundown from the moment Jackson Meredith bulled his way into my office. "So," I concluded. "What's the possibility this guy's wife is still alive? Who the hell is he, because Heather's having a hell of a time finding information on him, and who referred him to me?"

He was making notes as I talked. After I stopped, he continued to write for a few seconds. Then, he put his pen down, steepled his fingers and rested his chin on them.

"That's a lot of questions, and I'm not sure I can answer them." He held up an index finger. "First, the possibility that the police and the victim's father would misidentify her is weak. In order for me to believe they had the wrong body, and someone deliberately misidentified it . . . well, now you're talking conspiracy. Secondly,

I've never heard of Jackson Meredith, but I can look him up and get back to you. And, finally, I have no idea who sent him to you."

"Okay, Quince, anything you can do will be appreciated, especially the dirt on Meredith."

He did the steepled finger thing again, only this time, his almond-shaped eyes focused on me like a laser drill.

"You have issues with this guy?"

"Not exactly," I said. "I just have a gut feeling that he's more or less than he appears."

He laughed. "You mean he's not as rich as he appears, in which he's a poser, and you hate fakes, or he's richer than he appears, and since you don't particularly like rich people, you dislike him even more? Why did you even take him on as a client?"

Fair question, only my answer didn't make a whole lot of sense—I'm a sucker for a puzzle, the more it looks like it can't be solved, the more determined I am to solve it.

"This is like one of those locked room mysteries," I said. "If the guy's a nut, I'm gonna prove it, just to satisfy myself, and if he's not, I'm gonna find his wife." I shrugged

It was a simple answer to his question. Some would say a simple-minded answer. But, I'd taken quite a few cases because of the curiosity factor, and so far I'd not failed to come up with an answer. The look on Quincy's face, though, made me wonder if this was going to be a first.

Charles Ray

# SIX

It was 10:15 when I left Quincy's building. Sixteenth Street was just down the block, and I turned north on Sixteenth and drove up toward U Street, leaving the impersonal glass and steel sameness of Lobbyists' Row for the heterogeneity of the turn of the century architecture of the Westminster neighborhood, west of Howard University. A neighborhood of row houses in reds, blues, faded browns, and every color in between, that's coming back from the riots of the 60s, with coffee houses and bookstores as numerous as liquor stores and pawn shops these days, it's for me the thing that represents Washington, DC far better than even the white marble facades of the government buildings downtown.

The thing that keeps me coming to the area, though, is a little one-story brick building with faded and chipping white paint that sits in the middle of the block. The sign over the door gets a touch up every few years, and from what I've been told, the place gets a name change every ten years or so. Since I'd known it, though, it has just been 'Mom's'. It was an institution. People said Mom, the owner, head waitress, bookkeeper, and bouncer, came to DC from somewhere down south as a young woman, and ended up working in a restaurant because when she came in the early fifties, there were few jobs available for black women without college degrees. She had, however, a good head for business, and after only three years waiting tables, she owned the place. The next year, she married the cook, and has been dishing out soul food cooked in the traditional southern style since.

She has also more than doubled in size; probably from sampling her husband's cooking. Mom, whose real name I've never had the courage to inquire about, has to weigh at least 300 pounds. She stands about five-six, which makes her almost as wide as she is tall. But, anyone who thinks she's slow because of her size is in for a big surprise. Even though she waddles when she walks, she's amazingly spry for a person of her bulk.

I arrived at 11:00, delayed because of cross town traffic, parked my car at the corner and walked the half block. The bells over the entrance announced my entrance. A couple of swarthy laborers, and an elderly black man with snow white hair and a Santa-like beard and mustache combination, were the only seated customers, and they paid me no attention. The only other people I could see—I knew Mom's hubby was in the back at the stove—were Mom and a skinny little buy with skin the color of teak and dreadlocks. He wore faded jeans and an old army surplus field jacket. Mom stood in front of him with her ham-like hands on her hips. She wore a blue dress with white, red, and yellow dots that contained enough cloth to make a two-man tent. And, I didn't need to see the scowl on her face to know that she was pissed. Her voice, high-pitched for a woman her size, told me that.

"Who you think you are," she said. "Comin' all up in here an' tellin' me how to cook my food?"

The guy was less than half Mom's bulk and about an inch shorter, but he stood his ground, glaring up at her snarling face. He was either very brave, or very stupid—and, my money was on the latter.

"I'm not trying to tell you how to cook, ma'am," he said. "I was just saying that maybe you shouldn't fry so much of your food, or maybe use healthier oil for the things you do fry."

She poked a meaty finger at his face, causing him to take a step backwards.

"Now, you listen to me, you young pup. I been cookin' soul food since 'fore you was a gleam in your pappy's eye. You don't be comin' up in here tellin' me nothin' 'bout cookin', you hear me?"

"B-but, you should be thinking about your customers' health. All that fried food is just going to clog their arteries," he said. "Do you know that heart disease is one of the biggest killers of African-Americans?"

Mom came off her stool, hovering over the guy, who was now beginning to cringe a bit as if he thought she might hit him, and the look on her face said he wasn't far from right.

"You sayin' I killin' my customers, boy?" Her voice, usually deep and resonant, rose a full octave. "That what you sayin'?"

"W-well . . . n-no, I'm not saying you're killing your customers. You misunderstand me. I'm just saying that your cooking methods aren't contributing to their good health."

Mom's lips were quivering, and her clenched fists were trembling. She looked around the room. The Hispanic diners had their head down, focusing on their food. The old man was grinning, showing dark gaps in his mouth, clearly enjoying the show. Then, her eyes fell on me. Her smile was welcoming, but strained.

"Why don't we let one of my customers tell you if he think I be killin' folks with my food," she said. She pointed at me. "Al, honey, you eats here lots . . . you think my food be killin' you?"

Now, I'd found the tableau interesting, entertaining even, but the last thing I wanted to do was get between Mom and some health freak with a death wish.

"Not that I'm aware of," I said, hoping that would settle the issue.

But, the little guy was a true believer, whatever it was he believed in, and he just couldn't cut his losses and retreat. He turned, pointing a boney finger at me.

"Do you know what your cholesterol levels are?" he asked. "And, how much they're impacted by what you eat here?"

Well, that did it. The idiot had sucked me in by making it personal, and he'd overplayed his hand, because I *do* know my cholesterol levels, and the rest of my vital statistics as well. A holdover my army days is the annual physical. As a retired soldier, I get it done free every year at Walter Reed Medical Center on Georgia Avenue.

"As a matter of fact, friend," I said. "I do know my cholesterol levels. My HDL is 40, which is in the middle of the acceptable range, my LDL's 100, which is just to the right of mid-range, and my triglycerides are 110. I have a resting pulse rate of 72 beats per minute, and blood pressure of 117 over 70. Any more questions?"

He stood there looking at me with his mouth open and his eyes round like tiny saucers. Mom just leaned back against the counter with a smug look on her chubby face.

"You tell 'im, son," the old white haired man said. "Ain't nobody gone mess wit Mom's soul food."

That got a hearty laugh from Mom. "You tell 'em, Woody," she said. "Say, Al, you here for lunch?"

"Uh, yes, I'm meeting Buster."

"Aw, that's great. You two can test my Thanksgivin' special; it's gone be fried turkey, candy yams, and my special corn cake. And, I'm gone have sweet potato pie for dessert."

My mouth watered and my stomach rumbled at the thought.

"Sounds great," I said. "Make it two. I'm sure Buster will love it."

The dreadlocked diet monitor stood there looking perplexed at the direction the conversation had taken. Finally, he made a snorting sound, turned on his heels and stormed out, causing the bells to jangle instead of tinkle.

"Good riddance," Mom said. "Little runt come in here insultin' my food. Good think you come when you did. I's just 'bout to bust his head wit a skillet."

"I'm glad I came, then. Buster would have to take you in for assault if you did that."

"Aw, it'd be justifiable homicide. Ain't got no bidness comin' into a woman's kitchen and insultin' her food like that. Now, you gone and set yourself down. You want a cup of coffee?"

"I'll have some unsweetened iced tea, if you don't mind," I said.

She nodded and went behind the counter to get my tea and put in the order for the food. For a change I'd beaten Buster. Usually, when we eat at Mom's, he's there far enough ahead of me to be half finished with his food. I went to our usual table in the corner, with a good view of the street through the large plate glass window, and the entire dining area. I sat with my back to the wall. Mom brought a large water glass and a pitcher of tea. The ice inside caused beads of condensation on the outside of the clear glass pitcher. She filled the glass, put the pitcher in the center of the table and went back to her post near the cash register, where she perched her huge buttocks on a stool, where she sat looking out over her realm. All was again right with the world.

I was nearly half way through my first glass of tea when Buster came in. I'm just over six feet tall, but he tops me by at least an inch, and outweighs me by ten pounds, and none of it's fat. Before he became a DC cop, he'd been a star college football player. A knee injury kept him out of the NFL, so he turned to his second love, police work.

Shucking his blue pea coat, which he draped over the back of the other chair facing the street, he plopped himself down.

"Hey, bro," he said, sticking out his big hand. "You beat me here. What's up?"

Mom came over before I could answer.

"You want tea, Buster, or you drinkin' coffee?"

"Shoot," he said. "I been drinkin' that mud down at the precinct all mornin'. I think I'll be havin' a cup of your fine coffee, Mom."

She beamed a broad smile at him and ran her hand across his bald pate.

"You just tryin' to get in good wit me, ain't you? You ain't foolin' me, I know you done somethin' bad."

"Aw, come on, Mom, you know me. I'm always good."

"Yeah, even when you bad. I go git your coffee. Food be out in a few minutes."

She waddled off and came back a few seconds later with a large white mug with steam pouring out the top, which she sat in front of him. He lifted the mug, blew on it and took a sip.

"Hm, now that's some *good* coffee," he said, licking his lips. "You the best, Mom, and I mean that."

She 'humphed' and waddled back to the counter.

"So, bro, I got the accident report you asked about," he said when she was out of earshot. "I looked over it. It was just a routine one-car crash; chick was goin' too fast and her car hit a patch of ice and lost control. Smashed into a utility pole, and she got her chest crushed. Dead at the scene. End of story."

He took two sheets of folded paper from his pants pocket and passed it to me. It was full of the jargon cops use to fill out incident reports, but it said essentially what he'd just said.

"Why you interested in a car crash?" he asked. "You workin' for the insurance company or something?"

Before I could answer him, Mom came to the table carrying a large wooden tray laden with plates. The plates were laden with food, and the aromas coming from that food starting my salivary glands working overtime again. She put a plate filled with large slabs of dark meat, candied yams and dark red beans swimming in their juice, and two smaller plates; one with two squares of golden brown cornbread, and the other with a huge slice of potato pie with marshmallows melted into the top, in front of each of us.

"Enjoy your food, boys," she said. "Let me know what you think of it."

"I don't know 'bout the taste," Buster said. "But it smell like a little piece of heaven."

That earned him another pat on the head before she walked off, her wide hips swaying from side to side.

Conversation was put on hold until we'd sampled the turkey. Roast turkey might be the tradition for many people at Thanksgiving, but deep fried turkey is the way to go. The outside is brown and crispy, and the meat underneath the skin is so tender it just falls off the bone, and fairly melts in your mouth. If you can do it without burning down your house, it's definitely the way to go with the big birds.

After sampling everything but the pie, we sat back and patted our stomachs.

"I'll have to run ten miles to work this off," I said.

"Yeah, but it's worth it," Buster said. "Now, while I eat, why don't you tell me why you're interested in a routine traffic fatality."

Buster talks street trash a lot, but when he's a mind to, he can sound like a Rhodes scholar, which he almost was, if he hadn't missed an exam to play in a championship game, and he's got one of the sharpest minds of any cop I've ever known.

"Her husband thinks the body in that car wasn't her," I said. "He's hired me to prove it."

He paused with his fork halfway to his mouth.

"You're kidding. According to the dude I talked to at Montgomery County Police headquarters, the victim's father ID'ed her. The body wasn't disfigured either, so they're pretty convinced it was a legit ID."

"Yeah, I know that, but this guy sounded pretty convincing, too."

"Dude's crazy if you ask me. He's just in denial. You know how that can be." Then, he realized the significance of what he'd said. "I mean, it's pretty normal for some people to deal with grief by denying it, you know."

Realizing he couldn't walk that horse back into the barn, he turned his attention back to his food. I knew that he knew that it still hurt. Yeah, my mind had tried to deny that my wife and son had had their lives snuffed out by a stupid shit of a truck driver who'd run a stop sign. But when I saw them lying there on those sterile metal slabs, it was real; there was no denying it.

"Look, Jackson Meredith struck me as an asshole, but he didn't seem like a crazy man."

He stopped eating again. "Jackson Meredith? He wouldn't be Jackson Meredith of WheMer Developers, would he?"

"Yeah, you know him?"

"Hell yeah. Ain't a cop in DC don't know Black Jack Meredith."

"What . . . he have a rap sheet?"

"No, it's not like that. I mean, the guy's got a reputation as a hard ass; hell, what I hear is nobody likes him. But, I know his name from his partner, dude named Noah Whelan. He's supposed to have skipped a month or so back, if I remember, took a few million bucks of company money with him."

"Yeah, I saw something about that. Any idea where this Whelan character is?"

"Naw, way I heard it, is the feds tracked him as far as Miami International Airport. He took a flight from Reagan National, got off in Miami, and now he's in the wind. Not a trace of him after he got off that plane and left the airport."

"Shit, how does someone just disappear?"

"In Florida? Easier than you think. He could've had contacts there, got a ride down to the Keys, and got on a mosquito boat. Drug runners use 'em to run their product into the country. They could've run him down to Costa Rica or one of the other Central American countries. With all the money he had he could buy his way to just about anywhere."

Well, that was a dead end. Besides, it didn't have anything to do with finding Caroline Meredith. Of course, I was still my normal curious self.

"Why do they call this guy Black Jack?" I asked.

"Apparently, he's hooked on the card game. At least, that's what I heard. They say he goes to Vegas every month, or overseas, and he's dropped a ton of dough."

A gambling addict. A piece of information I filed away. I wasn't sure what I'd do with it, but it was something I hadn't known. I'd have Heather look into it just for the hell of it.

"So," he continued. "You really gonna try and find this guy's wife? You've had some wacky cases, my man, but this one takes the cake."

"Hey, the man's paying top dollar, and I already told him I don't guarantee results. But, I will give it my best effort."

"Good luck with that," he said. "Now, I'm gonna give my best effort on this potato pie."

Charles Ray

# SEVEN

After the pie, and another glass of tea, I paid the tab and drove back to the office. Heather looked up when I walked in and sniffed the air.

"Whew, you smell like you bathed in cooking oil," she said.

"I had fried turkey for lunch," I said.

She didn't have to say anything after that; her expression said it all. Heather's not a big fan of fried food, or much else of what I eat for that matter. I *like* fried food, I eat often at McDonalds, Burger King, and Popeye's, while she prefers the salad bar at Olive Gardens—when she eats out, which is seldom. It's a subject we both try to avoid, because we're both stuck in our ways.

"I found out that Jackson Meredith's

nickname is Black Jack," I said. "Want to know why?"

"Because he has a gambling addiction," she said.

"Aw, that was just a lucky guess."

She smirked and opened her notebook.

"No, that was the result of careful research," she said.

She'd learned of Meredith's frequent trips to Vegas and that his recent trip to Hong Kong had included a three-day side trip to Macao to visit the casinos there. He had a habit all right, and it was a big one—to the tune of twenty-five to fifty thousand bucks a month; and that, she said, was just an estimate. Gambling addiction and Vegas spelled trouble.

"I would wager that he's in hock big time to either a bookie or a loan shark."

"That's the rumor," she said. "Or, was the rumor until a few months ago when he paid his debt. Of course, I hear he's in the process of running up more."

"I knew there was something unsavory about this guy the minute I laid eyes on him."

She snapped the notebook shut. "Okay, so your instincts are still good," she said. "But, none of this has anything to do with his belief that his wife's not dead."

"Good point. I'll focus on that. By the way, Buster and Quincy think our client's delusional and we're crazy for taking him on."

She shrugged. Truth be told, Heather's

almost as intrigued by puzzles as I am, she's just not as vocal about it. "Anyway, we'll give it our best shot. I think I'll start with Caroline's father. Do you have his address?"

She did. Matt Donahue lived on Old Hundred Road, Maryland Route 109, north of Germantown itself, but inside its postal district. She pulled up a map on her laptop and showed me the route from downtown. I looked at my watch. It was going on 2:00 pm, which gave me just enough time, I figured, to drive there, talk to Caroline's father and get home in time to cook dinner. I was pushing myself not to continually refer to her as 'the victim,' as was the case in the police reports. In my mind that sterile phrase dehumanizes. The individual's life has already been taken. There's no sense taking the humanity away as well.

Before leaving, I reminded Heather to dig deeper into Meredith's gambling problem.

Charles Ray

# EIGHT

Thanks to Heather's advice on a route, the trip wasn't as unpleasant as I'd feared it might be. The usual way for folks to get from DC to Germantown and points northwest is to take I-270, which spears north from the I-495 Beltway up through Gaithersburg, Germantown and ending at I-70 in Frederick. The rising housing costs in the DC area and the expansion of the suburbs means that a lot of the District's government employees are now forced to live farther and farther out, with a significant number as far north as Frederick, in Frederick County, Maryland. This means that I-270 is a parking lot southbound in the mornings, and the same going north in the afternoon.

Following Heather's suggestion, I drove the route I normally take to get home; Whitehurst Freeway to Canal Road and up to

River Road, then Travillah Road north to Darnestown Road, which is close to Great Seneca Highway, which goes northwest to Germantown. The traffic this way is heavy, too, but nothing compared to I-270, and when you get past Route 124 in Gaithersburg, it really lightens up. It's really a nice drive, with a few forested areas and scattered housing developments; not the sprawl you see in some of the inner suburbs. The red, brown, yellow, and gold of autumn foliage, set against a dull blue sky is the stuff of great landscape photography.

Germantown is a modest sized northern Maryland town. My route didn't take me through the old part of town, which still has buildings with wrought iron railings on balconies and decorative brick fronts. Instead, I drove through the western edge of Germantown, where shopping malls, garages, schools, government buildings, and new housing developments give it a look not unlike Rockville and Gaithersburg to the south; a place where the drones of Washington, DC's sterile office buildings go after work to immerse themselves in the sameness of suburban living, which includes mowing the lawn, walking the dog, and barbecuing in the back yard.

As Maryland Route 109 approaches Frederick County, a less affluent place than Montgomery County, the suburban look gives way to a more rural motif. Gone are the rubber stamped, overpriced houses in the homeowner association-managed communities, replaced by more modest looking dwellings—with the occasional rich man's house tucked behind towering hardwood trees and high brick walls—that reflect the individual taste or economic level of the owners. It's not unusual to see a rusted out pickup on concrete blocks, or rotting tires nesting in the ragged grass of someone's lawn. Farther north, the farms begin. Mostly dairy farms, with large red sided, silver roofed barns and herds of placidly grazing black and white Herefords. You have to keep an eye out as you drive, to keep from rear-ending slow moving farm machinery that claims equal access to the road.

Matt Donahue's place wasn't exactly on Old Hundred Road; it was on a one-lane macadam road that ran northwest off Old Hundred Road. It was a small, three bedroom rambler, white with red trim, and a green roof. The two-car garage was detached. His lawn was neatly trimmed and bordered with fall-blooming flowers. A small aluminum flagpole sat in the center of the lawn to the right of the front entrance, with the American flag flapping proudly in the afternoon breeze. Over the center of his roof I could see the dark rounded top of Sugar Loaf Mountain in the distance.

I pulled into the driveway, stopping a few

feet from the garage door. I had to walk across a small patch of lawn to get to the walk. Despite the lateness of the season, the grass was soft and cushiony beneath my feet. I stepped up onto the concrete pad that served as a front porch and rang the bell.

Even if I'd not known in advance, I would have pegged Matt Donahue as ex-military.

According to the information Heather had dug up on him, he was 79 years-old, but except for the extra lines on his forehead, and the scattering of white in his close-cropped brown hair, cut tight on the side in accordance with Marine Corps regulations, he could have passed for someone in his late forties. He stood erect, shoulders back and chest out, and looked me right in the eye. He was nearly my height, and maybe ten or fifteen pounds lighter, but his shoulders nearly filled the doorway. When he spoke, I could hear the cadence of the drill ground in his voice. "Something I can do for you, mister?"

The way he stared at me, not blinking, not hostile, but like I was something strange attached to his shoe and he'd not quite decided whether to ignore it or scrape it off. This was not a man to try running a game on. He'd probably seen them all; and run quite a few of them himself.

"Mr. Donahue, Matt Donahue?" I said. He nodded. "My name's Al Pennyback. I'm a private investigator, and I've been hired to look into your late daughter's accident."

I pulled out my ID and held it out to him. He didn't take it, but looked at it for a long time, before locking gaze with me again.

"I thought that was done with," he said. "Caroline, unfortunately, was driving a bit too fast for the road conditions and rammed into a light pole . . . end of story. The insurance company decided they don't want to pay damages?"

I was tempted to let him think I was working for the insurance company, but since I didn't know which company it was, or whether or not they paid claims when the insurer was at fault, I knew it would backfire. Besides, something inside me wanted to be straight up with this guy.

"I'm not working for the insurance company, Mr. Donahue. Your son-in-law, Jackson Meredith, hired me."

His expression darkened, and more lines appeared on his furrowed brow. "Why does that son of a bitch want the crash investigated? He must have a big policy that's hesitating to pay because the cops are saying the accident was Caroline's fault. Well, fuck him and the horse he rode in on."

Meredith had said his father-in-law didn't like him. From the look on Donahue's face, I was thinking he'd understated it. The man seemed to purely hate him.

"Sir, I know this a sensitive subject," I said. "And, I don't like intruding on you during your time of grief; but, if you'd let me come in and speak to you for just a few minutes, I'd be mighty obliged."

He continued to glare, not speaking for several seconds. Then, he stepped back in the doorway and inclined his head.

"You ever in the military?" he asked as I walked past him into a sparsely furnished, but inspection-neat living room.

"Yes sir, I was in the army. Twenty years."

He let a half smile lighten his expression. "Thought so, I can tell. You're polite. Most civilians ain't polite at all. And, you carry yourself like a man knows what he's about. Ain't seen no civilians with that degree of self-confidence—arrogance, but not self-confidence. Ain't the same thing at all. Me, I was in the Marines. I did thirty."

He pointed at an old, but serviceable couch. The doilies on the arms were a bit yellowed with age, but aligned precisely. The coffee table was centered on the couch, with an ash tray set in the center. An easy chair, with doilies identical to those on the sofa, sat to the left, at a right angle to the sofa. I sat near the easy chair, which he sat in.

"Twenty years in," I said. "You must've been in Korea."

"Hell, son, I turned 18 the year the Japs hit Pearl Harbor. Went down to the recruiting office in Germantown and enlisted the first chance. I was at Iwo Jima and some of the other islands—they was all bad, but Iwo was the worst. Got me a Purple Heart for landing on that fucking piece of volcanic rock. When Tojo surrendered, we all breathed a sigh of relief, thinking that kind of war was over, but then the damn commies crossed the 38th Parallel, and I got sent to Korea. I was a gunny by then, in Force Recon. My unit was with the army and Marines at the Frozen Chosin. I never thought I'd see anything worse than Iwo Jima until I spent a winter being chased by Chicoms from that frozen piece of hell. I retired in 1971, been living here in this house ever since. What about you? You see action while you were in the army?"

"Yeah, I got the tail end of Vietnam," I said. "I was in Special Forces, so I got to vacation in a few other nice spots before I retired."

He nodded and his face relaxed. We'd been like two strange dogs meeting for the first time. They sniff at each other's butts to establish identity and intentions. Old soldiers are like that. The abbreviated recitation establishes credentials. True warriors will briefly mention their battles without going into detail—the name, place or date is enough. It establishes that the two strangers in fact belong to the same brotherhood. I'd been accepted. Now, all I had to do was avoid doing something to erase that acceptance.

"So, that no-good son-in-law of mine hired you," he said. "Is there something about the accident that's strange? What's his angle?"

His question put me in a tricky situation. Normally, I keep information about clients pretty close, but this was a fellow veteran, moreover, one who'd been through the hell of two wars. I couldn't see myself doing or saying anything to deceive him, so I broke the cardinal rule of detective work. "You're going to find this crazy," I said. "But, your son-in-law believes your daughter is still alive, and he's hired me to prove it."

For a few seconds he just sat there looking at me. Then, he leaned back in his chair and began laughing. He laughed so hard, tears welled from his eyes, and he folded his arms over his stomach. Finally, his laughter subsided, and he leaned forward, putting his hands on his knees.

"I knew that little shit was a turd, but I never thought he was crazy to boot. Son, I identified my daughter's body. I don't know what old Black Jack's been smoking, but it must be pretty powerful."

"Can you tell me, Mr. Donahue, just so I can say I investigated thoroughly, why you cremated your daughter before her . . . husband came back to the states?"

He looked at me through narrowed eyes. "First off, why don't you call me Matt? Can't be having all that formality between two veterans, now can we? I'll tell you why I did it, and I'll leave it to you to decide whether or not you want to tell that pecker head. I did it because I didn't want him anywhere my daughter when she was alive, but she had a mind of her own, and I couldn't do a damn thing about it. But, I could decide whether or not he'd be at her funeral. If I'd waited, he might have been able to exercise his right as her husband, and . . . well, there's just no way I was gonna do that, get it. I knew it'd piss him off. It'll piss him off even more if you tell him why I did what I did, so go ahead if you want."

Damn, he really did hate his son-in-law. I wasn't sure it was a good idea to tell my client this. Of course, I didn't like my own client that much either. I was conflicted. That, however, Donahue didn't need to know.

"I'll give it some thought," I said. "What can you tell me about Meredith—I mean, other than the fact that you don't like him? What, for instance, was their relationship like?"

A look . . . I couldn't tell if it was sadness or anger . . . flashed across his craggy face.

He shook himself. "Say, where are my manners?" he said. "Would you like something to drink . . . coffee, or maybe something a bit stronger? I got some good sipping whiskey."

"Coffee would be fine," I said. "I have a long drive this afternoon, and you know how traffic can be around here."

"Actually, I don't do much driving except to go into town once a month to get supplies, or over to Fort Meade to see the doctor. I got a bad ticker." He stood. "You wait right here, I'll bring us some coffee."

He went toward the back of the house, where I assumed the kitchen and dining room to be. While I waited, I did what people usually do when they're in someone else's house for the first time, and what I as a PI do all the time, I snooped. I checked out the books in a bookcase on the wall opposite the sofa; mostly war novels, along with some map and history books. There were pictures on the wall next to the bookcase, about ten, 5 by 7 in black wooden frames, two color photos of Donahue and a beautiful woman with long, brown hair, and a little girl I assumed was Caroline, two of Donahue and the woman alone, four of Donahue and the little girl at different ages, a photo of the girl at what appeared to be about twelve or thirteen with a gangly, pimply-faced boy, and a photo of her as an older teenager with hair like the older woman. I assumed the teenager was Caroline. She looked like her mother. I took particular note of the fact that there were no photos of Caroline and her husband.

Moving on around the room, I came to another bookcase. This one had a photo of a younger Donahue in his Marine Corps full dress uniform. He had six rows of ribbons on his chest, more fruit salad than Old Country Buffet, an Expert Marksman's Medal, and a parachutist badge. I looked closely and saw that his was a Master Parachutist's Badge, signifying that he'd made over 100 jumps, and a little gold star on it, that meant he'd done a combat jump. In a little case on the first shelf there was the Distinguished Service Cross, a Silver Star with two Oak Leaf Clusters, and a Purple Heart with four Oak Leaf Clusters. The little bronze leaf clusters indicated additional awards of the medals, and the medals themselves are for heroism under fire, except the Purple Heart, which is awarded to service members injured in battle. This guy was the real deal.

I was still looking at the medals when he came back into the room. He cleared his throat to let me know he was back. I turned away from the medal display to see that his cheeks were red, and he looked embarrassed, as if dreading that I would say something about them. I knew the feeling, so I said nothing. I walked over to him and took the large red mug with the globe, anchor and chain of the Marine Corps crest emblazoned on it that he held out for me. I went back to the sofa and sat, sipping my coffee, waiting for him to answer the question he'd ducked by offering me a drink.

He resumed his place in the easy chair, sipping his coffee and looking at me.

Finally, he sighed heavily. "I never understood what she saw in him," he said. "She was bright and beautiful; could've had any man she wanted, but she had to fall in love with that . . . scoundrel. When she told me they were . . . together . . . I tried to talk her out of it, but she was as headstrong as her mother."

"Did they have any kind of marital problems that you were aware of?"

He glanced toward the photos on the wall.

"No, as far as I can tell they got along just fine."

"You mind me asking, Matt, why don't you like your son-in-law?"

"Oh, it's not just one thing," he said. "When Caroline first brought him home, he struck me as too smug, you know. It was like he was looking down his nose at the world. The more I knew him, though, the more I got the feeling . . . that turkey's got a mean streak. He's all smooth on the surface, but I saw too many like him in the Corps; guys that love to inflict pain. I tell you, I was worried he'd abuse my little girl."

"Did he ever do that?"

He hesitated, a finger in the air. "Abuse her? No, at least, not that I know," he said. He looked down at the floor. "I think if she'd been getting abused, I would've known, you know."

That hesitation, and him repeating my question set of a little alarm bell in my head. He was holding something back. Had Meredith been physically abusing his wife? That's something most families don't like to face or own up to. But, Meredith struck me as the type who would confront anyone he thought was hurting his daughter. Something didn't add up, but I didn't want to push too hard; especially if it had nothing to do with Meredith claim that his wife was still alive; a claim that, from Donahue's statement, was looking more and more like an obsession.

"Sometimes people hide things like that," I said. "I don't know, maybe it's shame, the victim blaming herself; there's even the Stockholm Syndrome where victims begin to identify with their attackers. She might have kept it from you>"

"No, I don't think so. She told me everything. Caroline and me, we were close, especially after her mother died. Hell, except for Sheldon, we only had each other."

"Who is Sheldon?" I asked.

He pointed at the picture of the girl and the gawky boy.

"Sheldon Logan, he's my nephew, well, actually my wife's nephew," he said. "He was her younger sister's child. He and Caroline sort of grew up together. He used to come up here from North Carolina during school vacations and in the summer. When Rebecca, that's my wife; when she died, Sheldon's mom let him move up with us. The two of them were like brother and sister."

"Where's Sheldon now? Did he go back to North Carolina?"

"No; him and Caroline finished high school together and both got into University of Maryland. Caroline got that useless English degree, but Sheldon did pre-med and then went on to medical school. He's an intern in Castle Creek Hospital over in Damascus."

I made a mental note to look Sheldon Logan up. Donahue might have truly believed that his daughter would tell him if her husband was abusing her, but I've heard stories of too many abusing women hiding their abuse from their families. Someone she considered a brother, though; she just might have let something slip to.

You might well ask what the hell any of this had to do with finding out whether or not she was dead. It didn't. But, if Jackson Meredith had been abusing his wife, it might explain his inability to accept her death. Abuse is often, almost always, about exercising power and control over the victim. By dying while he was away, she'd escaped his control, and maybe his mind was having difficulty accepting it. If I could prove it, I could rub his face in it. It wouldn't bring her back, but there would be a certain justice in him paying for the privilege of being outed as a wife beater.

Donahue sat there holding his coffee mug in both hands. I noticed that his hands were shaking and his eyes glistened with unshed tears. I felt like a heel. The man had lost his only child, a daughter who had, I was convinced, suffered at the hands of her husband. Well, she would have justice. It wasn't likely the authorities would prosecute Meredith, what with the victim being dead and all, but his reputation would suffer if it became public, and my assessment was that his reputation meant a lot to him. Yes, Jackson Meredith would suffer like this old man sitting across from me was suffering.

"Matt, I am truly sorry for your loss," I said. "And, I'm sorry for coming here and bringing it all up again."

"I'm not holding it against you, Al. You're just doing your job. Can't say I think too much of your employer, but just because he's a shit, don't mean you shouldn't do what you're paid to do."

That made me feel worse. I would have expected him to rail at me, curse, or toss me out of his house. Instead, he was forgiving me.

I felt like shit as I shook his trembling hand.

Charles Ray

# NINE

I felt like shit on the drive home, which, thanks to the fact that I was driving against the rush hour flow, was mercifully short. It was 5:30 when I pulled up in front of the farmhouse. The sky was already turning purple. Long shadows of the nearby trees lay across the yard.

Just as I was getting out of my car, Sandra pulled in next to me. She was home early.

"Hey," I said as she got out of her car. "I thought you were helping with the Thanksgiving play at your school."

"Rehearsals went so well, we let the kids go early. You're getting here pretty late. Anything interesting happening in your missing person case?" She smiled as she asked. She still thought I was chasing a ghost.

"Come on inside. I'll tell you while I fix supper."

We shucked our jackets, and took a little time to warm up. The temperature, though a bit warm at midday, had plummeted around four in the afternoon, and just the short walk from the cars to the front door had left our hands tingling.

While I chopped some onions and jalapenos in preparation for making a pot of my five-alarm chili, Sandra poured two glasses of red wine. I reminded her that we'd be drinking beer with the chili, which earned me a pout, followed by a wine-flavored kiss. She left me to do my magic and went out to the living room to sip her wine and listen to classical music on PBS.

After she left, I put the glass of wine in the fridge and took out a bottle of Dos Equis, which I opened and put on the counter next to the cutting board. No way was I going to spoil my chili with the taste of wine.

I started rice going in the cooker, whipped up a batch of cornbread with sweet corn and onions and put it in the oven, and then started on the chili. That involves dusting chunks of beef with black pepper and a pinch of salt and putting them in a pot with a tablespoon of vegetable oil to brown. I then add more black pepper, a pinch of salt, chili powder, and a teaspoon of cumin and mix it thoroughly. Next comes a can of tomato paste and three cans of water with the chopped onions and jalapenos. I stir all that together, cover it, put it on low heat, and sip my beer while it simmers.

The cornbread is done first. I take that out of the oven, cut it into squares and put them on a plate. The chili and rice finish about the same time. I put a couple of tablespoons of rice in a bowl, and cover it with chili. Two bowls of that on the table, two fresh Dos Equis, and the cornbread in the middle of the table, and chow's on.

"Okay, babe," I called. "Let's eat."

Sandra had finished her wine. She frowned at the bottle of beer near her bowl of chili, and I frowned back, so she just shrugged. Sandra's a Midwesterner, and is just learning to appreciate the finer points of southern and southwestern cooking. She grew up in a town where restaurants refused to carry tabasco sauce for fear it would burn a customer who would then sue them. Where I grew up, most places carried three or four different brands of hot sauce, just in case.

I will give her credit, though. She's a trooper. The first time she ate my five-alarm chili, her face turned red and her eyes watered. She coughed so hard, she blew phlegm from her nose. Now, she can eat my chili with nothing worse than red cheeks.

She put the first spoonful into her mouth, following it immediately with a huge bite of cornbread—I'd taught her that bread or rice is much better than water to deal with pepper burn in the mouth. The burn's caused by the oils in the pepper seeds, and water only spreads it around, while bread or rice absorbs it. She's a quick learner. She got the first mouthful down and only had the slightest pink tinge to her cheeks. She lifted her beer and toasted me with a smirk.

We both had seconds, and as a reward to her, I took the stashed glass of wine from the refrigerator, poured her another, and went with her to the living room, where we huddled in our usual place on the couch with the radio at low volume playing love songs from the fifties.

While we listened, I brought her up to date on the case, including my visit to Matt Donahue and my suspicion that my client was a wife beater. I shared my theory that he was a control freak who was pissed that his wife had the gall to die when he wasn't around, and he was using me and my investigation to inflict pain on her father, or maybe he was just a psycho, and his tormented mind couldn't accept that his wife had escaped his control. At any rate, I told her, I was going to do all I could to get proof of his misdeeds, and the neat thing is that he'd be paying me to do it.

When I finished, she sat there looking at the deep red liquid in her glass for a long time. Then, she took a sip, put the glass down and turned to me. "You've got to nail that son of a bitch, Al," she said.

Charles Ray

# TEN

Fridays are strange in the DC area. Being a large southern town in character, and historically, it's never been a frenetic place like New York City or Chicago, or even large southern cities like Dallas, Atlanta, or New Orleans. It's always reminded me of more sedate places, like Savannah or Charleston. You'd think, though, that being the seat of the federal government, there'd be a certain level of energy to the place. Think again. Except for the insane traffic, caused mainly by the fact that most people in the area, natives and outsiders alike, seem to forget how to drive as soon as they're within fifty miles of I-495, the pace of DC is slow to moderate, except on weekends when the government buildings go silent—except for emergency staffs and workaholics—and Friday. On Friday, a lot of people take leave to get an unsanctioned three-day weekend, or get a jump on the weekend traffic heading north and south. So, even though the traffic that's left is still a pain in the ass, the buildings are minimally staffed, causing a kind of quiet to settle over the city.

As a result, my drive to work was relatively quiet. No incidents of road rage, no one cutting in front of me, only to change back to their original lane a few seconds later, so idiot suddenly slowing down in front of me to gawk at a fender bender on the other side of the street. I was feeling pretty good when I walked into the office.

Heather was at her desk, her fingers fairly flying over her laptop keyboard, with a cup of fragrant tea and her notebook at her left elbow. She looked up and smiled brightly as I shrugged out of my jacket.

"How'd your visit with Mr. Donahue go?" she asked.

I filled her in. Her reaction wasn't as harsh as Sandra's, but her brow wrinkled and her cheeks turned red.

"So, you see, I think our client's got problems beyond his gambling addiction," I said.

"What are you going to do about it?"

"If the victim, Caroline, was still alive, I'd be trying to get enough evidence to prosecute the bastard," I said. "But, without a live victim, and the fact that he had nothing to do with her death, I doubt the District would charge him. So, I guess the only thing left is to get some solid proof, and then publicize it to shame him. And, the nice thing is, he'll be paying us to do it."

She mulled that over for all of five seconds.

"Let's do it," she said. "We can start with the fact that he's abusive to his employees as well."

"What? How do you know that?"

"Hey, you said dig deep, so I did. I found a labor complaint; a discharged employee filed a discrimination action against WheMer for wrongful termination. I made a few calls, and got his number." She wrote a name and number on a Post-It note and handed it to me. "He has an interesting story to tell."

I looked at the note. It had the name, Aaron Cooper, and an address on Belmont Road, near Woodley Park, and just south of Rock Creek.

"Do you have his phone number? Could you call and ask if he'll talk to me?"

"I already did . . . yesterday," she said. "I figured you'd want to see him right away. He said he's free all morning."

I folded the note and put it in my shirt pocket. Since I was already out of my jacket, I went into my office and spent ten minutes deleting the useless junk from my email inbox—which was everything. I never get anything useful, but I follow Heather's advice and clean out my inbox every day to keep it from getting overloaded. After getting that little chore out of the way, I put my jacket back on and went back outside into the chilly morning air.

There are a number of ways to get to the Woodley Park area from downtown, and none of them are easy. The most scenic and pleasant, though, is to get on the Rock Creek and Potomac Parkway near the Lincoln Memorial, and follow it until you get to Massachusetts Avenue just south of Rock Creek. Rock Creek has carved a deep channel in the earth, and once you're past Pennsylvania Avenue, it's like being in another world. The hubbub of the District is way above your head and muffled by the lush foliage and thick stands of trees lining the creek. On a chilly November morning, it was pleasant to drive through a world of green, brown, red, orange, and yellow, with only the whishing sound of my tires on the concrete for sound.

At Massachusetts Avenue, I turned right off the parkway, and immediately left onto Belmont Road.

Aaron Cooper's house was a small red-brick colonial set back from the street and surrounded by stately oak trees. The driveway ended at a one-car garage.

A skinny, pale-faced guy, about a foot shorter than me, wearing faded jeans and a

Washington Redskins' sweat shirt, answered the doorbell. He brushed a lank mop of reddish hair from in front of his blue eyes and blinked up at me.

"Yes, may I help you?"

"Are you Aaron Cooper?" I asked.

He blinked again.

"Uh, yeah. Say, are you Al Pennybaker, the PI whose office called me yesterday?"

I showed him my ID. "It's Pennyback," I said. "Hope I'm not interrupting anything important."

He stepped aside for me to enter. "No, you're not interrupting anything. I'm . . . between jobs right now."

The living room was furnished in ritzy looking French Provincial, with lots of crystal vases on little tables, and small, ornately framed prints on the flowered walls. The sofa looked barely substantial enough to bear my weight, so I eased onto it carefully.

"You worked for WheMer Developers?"

"Yup, I worked there for six years," he said. "I was a site engineer."

He sat on a chair that I would have been leery of, but he seemed to be swallowed up by it. I guess at his size, the furniture was about right.

"I understand you left under . . . unfortunate circumstances?"

"You could say that." He laughed. "The son of a bitch fired me."

"I thought WheMer was a partnership.

Which partner fired you?"

He got up and headed toward a door near the back. "The prick that did all the firing," he said over his shoulder. "Jackson 'The Dickhead' Meredith liked canning people, so he was the one who gave people the ax when needed—not, mind you, that mine was needed. I'm still waiting for a decision on my wrongful termination suit. I'm gonna have a beer. You want one." The last came out just as he disappeared through the door.

"No thanks," I said, hopefully loud enough for him to hear.

It must have been. He came back a few seconds later drinking from a Budweiser can. His Adam's apple bobbed up and down as he chugged half the can in several gulps. He wiped foam from his lips as he resumed his seat.

"Okay, so where were we? Oh yeah, it was Jackson the prick who fired me. Or, did I already tell you that?"

"You did," I said. "Why did he fire you?"

He took another drink of beer, a more civilized sip this time.

"The letter he gave me said gross incompetence, but that was pure bullshit. He fired me because I wouldn't look the other way when he tried to get around the rules on a construction project—a construction project, by the way, that was one of Noah's pet projects. Noah Whelan was the other partner, and he was a nice guy."

"He's the one who embezzled money from the company and disappeared?"

"Don't you believe that," he said. He glared at me. "He's gone, okay, that's true, but you'll never get me to believe Noah stole any money. It's Jackson with the gambling problem. If anybody was gonna steal from the company, it'd be him."

This guy was just a low level employee, and clearly he didn't like Meredith, so I wasn't quite ready to lend too much credence to his opinion. On the other hand, he looked at me levelly over the rim of his beer can. He seemed pretty sure of what he was saying; and, he knew about Meredith's gambling.

"I don't know this guy Whelan, but running away is a pretty convincing sign of guilt. Why are you so sure he didn't take the money?"

"I just know him, is all. Besides, a few days before he disappeared, I happened to overhear him and Jackson arguing, and it was about money. Noah was mad as hell, and Jackson was red-faced and guilty looking. I remember that clearly, because it was the three days before Jackson canned me."

"About that, you said he fired you because you refused to bend the rules on some project. What was that about?"

"It's this warehouse complex out in Mount Airy," he said. "The workers are supposed to put in the forms for the load-bearing columns before pouring the concrete base, but

Jackson wanted the base poured right away. The workers resisted, and he threatened to fire 'em, so they went on strike. He then came to me and ordered me to hire scabs to come in and pour the concrete, and I refused—and, not just because I support union workers. You got to follow procedures on these projects or you can have compromise of structural integrity down the road, you know. Anyway, when I said no way, the shit head fired me. Told me to clear my desk and get the hell out."

"I guess he finally got his way on that one, eh?"

"Shit, I don't know, and frankly, right now, I don't give a rat's ass. I don't even want my job back. What I want is for the court to order that fucker to retract the letters he sent out to all the other developers in the area smearing my reputation. I have a degree in engineering, and the only job I can get right how is flipping burgers for minimum wage, or bussing tables for less. It's not right."

His eyes brimmed with tears, and he was clutching that can hard enough to make small dents in its side. If what he said was true, though, and I had no reason to doubt him, he had every reason to be upset. He was validating the image of Meredith my mind had constructed. Abusers tend to be bullies, who like exerting control over others, and they lash out at anyone who tries to resist them. It seemed that his wife was not his only victim.

I stood. "Well, best of luck with your case, and thanks for the information."

He was still sitting there, staring at the can, when I let myself out.

Charles Ray

# ELEVEN

I grabbed a roast beef sandwich and coffee to go at Panera Bread on Connecticut Avenue. Heather looked up in surprise when I set the still warm bag on the edge of her desk and began taking off my jacket.

"Is that actually a reasonably healthy lunch you have there?"

"Get off my case," I said. "I'd really like a Whopper with double fries, but we need to talk, so I'm making a major sacrifice here."

It's not that I'm a confirmed unhealthy eater. I just like burgers and fries. They taste good, they're quick to order . . . and, they taste good. Heather's more into bean sprouts and tofu, and she's always lecturing me about my eating habits.

"Okay," she said. "Sacrifice noted."

She took out her lunch. Looked like a mixture of bean sprouts and an assortment of plant products. I could smell the sesame seeds she sprinkled on it for flavor. Her ever present fragrant tea was already at hand. Next to the little plastic container of green stuff, she placed an open notebook. She was ready.

"Okay, here's how it seems to me," I said. I outlined my suspicions about Meredith, adding the information I'd gotten from Cooper.

"Our client's beginning to sound like a bad, bad boy," she said as she made notes. "Maybe we should give him his money back and drop this case."

"No way. This guy's a bully who needs to be brought down a peg. I figure making him pay for it just adds to his punishment."

She frowned, her brow wrinkling slightly. "I don't know, Al. Is this even legal? Or ethical? I mean, we're supposed to be working *for* our client, not against him."

She might as well have thrown a bucket of cold water in my face. That brought me up short. I'd been so focused on the fact that Jackson Meredith was a major league slime ball I'd forgotten that I was in a contractual relationship with the slime ball. Now, unlike lawyers, who are legally bound to maintain lawyer-client confidentiality—unless they're aware of a crime about to be committed—for private investigators, it's more of a moral-ethical obligation. No one's going to pull your license just because you divulge information about a client, but your chances of ever having another client after doing so are about as good as a snowball going through hell without losing weight. Same thing goes for working against your client's interests. Of course, if you discover your client's committed a crime, you're legally obligated to report it to the authorities. The situation I found myself in, though, was I only *suspected*, more like *felt* that my client had done wrong. The question was, did I cross some line by trying to prove it?

I believe strongly in honesty, and the first person you have to be honest with is yourself. Truly, I was convinced in my heart that Meredith was guilty of at least verbal abuse of his spouse, and probably other people as well. From Cooper's information, it was a good chance he was a physical abuser as well. But, exposing him wouldn't bring Caroline Meredith back, so was going after him worth it?

My contract with him required that I investigate the circumstances of his wife's death, and prove or disprove that she was still alive. My money was on her being dead. That was what Meredith was paying me to do, and I fully intended to do that. The alleged, suspected abuse was something I was doing on my own dime. Okay, I was doing it at the same time I did the other case, so technically you could probably say I my client was paying for it. But, if that was the case, he was getting a deal. Two cases for the price of one.

The ethical dilemma was what I had in mind to do with the information if I got it. Was it over the line to expose him publicly? I guess it depends on how you look at things. Should you act for the greater good, or for the good of one person? Would society benefit from knowing that a monster like Jackson Meredith was in their midst? I'd like to think so. Exposing him would hurt him, but it wasn't wrong to do so. In fact, it was right. Just as protecting his right to privacy was right. It's just that, in my view, protecting the greater number was a greater right.

I looked Heather directly in the eye and laid a hand on hers. "I will fulfill my contractual obligations to our client to the best of my ability," I said. "But, if in the course of doing that I become aware of some illegal or dangerous activity, I'm obligated to report it. So, while that might not be a comfortable situation for him, it's not exactly working against him."

She smiled. "I didn't say I wouldn't go along with it. I just wanted to know where you stood on the matter."

"So, you'll keep digging?"

"Like a ferret," she said.

The phone rang. Heather answered, and then looked at me strangely.

"What?"

"There's an FBI agent on the phone, and she says she'd like to come talk to you about Jackson Meredith."

Charles Ray

# TWELVE

FBI Special Agent Daisy Wentworth didn't look like any cop I'd ever met before. She was tiny. I pegged her at five-three and probably a hundred pounds. In the sky blue pant suit, and with her blonde hair pulled back exposing her forehead, she looked like a curious middle schooler. It was only the bulge of the 9mm pistol under her jacket that spoiled that image. Her partner, Special Agent William Smith, on the other hand, looked like a guy central casting would send to play a federal agent. At six-two, he topped me a bit, but was younger and fitter. His 190 pound frame was encased in a dark gray, almost blue, suit that must have come off the rack, because the jacket sleeve ended a half inch higher than it should have.

They showed up half an hour after I got off the phone with Wentworth, who happened to be the senior of the duo. She flashed her badge first, introducing herself and then her partner. He didn't say anything, just flashed his badge and stood there looking at me with a wooden expression.

Heather put her visitor's chair in my office to accommodate them. Wentworth took the one nearest the desk, while Smith sat on the one near my bookcase.

"Well, agents, what can I do for you?" I asked, before one of them could speak. It's important to establish control of the conversation. The first to speak, and preferably ask a question, can set the tone for the entire encounter. From the flicker of annoyance in Wentworth's eyes, I knew she'd had the same thing in mind, and I'd beat her to it.

I'll give her credit, though, she kept her cool. "Mr. Pennyback, it's come to our attention that you're working for Jackson Meredith, a partner in the firm, WheMer Developers." I nodded. "Can you share with us the nature of that investigation?"

Ordinarily I would have told her to pound sand. Unless the investigation's about some illegal activity, the cops can't compel a PI to divulge information on a client. At least, the local cops can't. I'm not sure what kind of authority feds have since 9/11, but I didn't think they'd hustle me off to Guantanamo if I refused to talk. On the other hand, you often have to give a little in order to get a little, and I was curious. Why was the FBI interested in Meredith? Probably to do with his partner absconding with company funds, but that didn't tell me why they'd want to know what a lowly PI was doing with him.

"I'll tell you, but you have to promise not to laugh," I said.

The stony expressions told me they had no intention of laughing, so I told them.

"Mr. Meredith hired me to look into his wife's auto accident." Still no expression. "He refuses to accept that she died in that wreck, and he's hired me to find her." That got a slight flicker of her lips, but she was good, she kept that stone-faced look.

"*Do* you think she's still alive?" she asked.

"Of course not. Her father identified the body."

"So, what have you found out?"

This was beginning to sound like an interrogation. I needed to regain at least some initiative.

"Nothing," I said. "Mind if I ask why you're interested in Meredith? I know you guys were investigating his partner, but—"

"That's right," she said. "We're investigating his partner's extortion of funds from the company, and subsequent disappearance. We were just interested in whether or not your . . . investigation had anything to do with that. Clearly it doesn't.

Sorry for taking up your time."

Damn! She was about to leave, and I'd gotten nothing. "I understand this Whelan guy ran away to Florida." I was fishing. "Why haven't you guys been able to find him? What's he doing, you think, hiding in the Everglades?"

"That's internal info—" Smith started to say, but Wentworth held a hand up, cutting him off.

"It's true, Whelan was last known to be at Miami International Airport," she said. "From there, he just dropped out of sight. But, we've scrubbed airport security camera footage and there's nothing showing him leaving that airport."

"Maybe he left on a charter flight, or on a private plane," I offered.

"Wentworth," Smith said. "This is against protocols."

"I think Mr. Pennyback might be able to help us, Smith," she said. She looked at me. "Can I trust you?"

"If you mean trust me not to go blabbing FBI secrets to the world, of course you can."

"This is on you, Wentworth," Smith said.

"I'll take that chance," she said. "If you're nervous about it, why don't you wait outside? That way, if things go south, you can say you knew nothing about it."

He looked conflicted. "Hell, we've been partners too long," he said. "If you go down, we both go. I'll stay."

"Okay," Wentworth said. "Here's the deal. We don't think Whelan flew out of Miami, because we have our doubts he ever flew *to* Miami in the first place. We think someone resembling Whelan took a flight from DC, using his ID, and then ditched it when they got there."

"So, where's Whelan, then?"

The two agents shared a look.

"Good question, Mr. Pennyback," Wentworth said finally. "We're hoping you can help us answer it."

All right, now we were getting somewhere.

"I'll do whatever I can, but I need to know a bit more about this case."

Smith frowned at me, but Wentworth just smiled. She was one smart lady. I wasn't just fishing. The more I know about a case going in, the fewer blind alleys I chase useless leads down. She understood that, so she gave me the background on the case. I'm sure she held a few things back. I would have done the same thing. But, I'm also sure she told me what she thought I'd need to know.

Jackson Meredith had called the DC police On October 14 to report that his partner, Noah Whelan, was missing, and had been for four days. Since the required 72 hours had passed, he was allowed to file a missing person's report, and had been interviewed. During the interview, he mentioned that a large amount of money from the firm's cash account was also missing, five million to be exact, and that he was worried that maybe his partner had been kidnapped and forced to give someone the money. When the cops discovered that a Noah Whelan had taken an American Airlines flight out of Reagan National Airport on October 9, bound for Miami, they called in the FBI.

The FBI immediately contacted their field office in Miami. Examination of surveillance camera footage, and interviews with staff, car rental companies, and taxi drivers left them with zero. No one had seen or heard of a Noah Whelan at the Miami airport. They'd also done a thorough investigation at National. According to Wentworth, there were fleeting images of an individual roughly matching Whelan in height and build, but whose face was obscured by the bill of a baseball cap, so a positive ID couldn't be made. Ticket counter personnel and the TSA security folks confirmed that someone named Noah Whelan, with proper ID, ticket and boarding pass, had been through their stations on October 9, and the boarding records indicated that Noah Whelan had boarded his flight. From there, the trail disappeared.

They'd assumed Whelan might have had a contact waiting for him somewhere in the airport, and had either taken a private flight, or gotten a ride with someone. But, the Miami field office had beaten the bushes and come up with nothing. There'd been nothing on any of the surveillance cameras in Miami showing the individual from Washington. Wentworth and Smith conceded that this could have meant that Whelan ditched the disguise as soon as he got off the plane, but it didn't explain him not showing up on even one camera. They'd begun to smell a rat, but they'd concluded that Meredith was the cagey type from their first interview with him when they'd taken the case, so had been reluctant to go at him for fear he'd bolt.

When I asked why they'd taken so long to think Meredith might be up to something, Wentworth laughed.

"When we train at Quantico," she said. "They tell us to trust our instincts. But, after getting beat up by U.S. Attorneys who just want hard evidence, you start to mistrust your gut, you know. The first time we met with Meredith, I thought he was off, but he was reporting a missing partner, so I wrote it off to nerves. I didn't notice at first, either, how he slowly introduced the missing money into the conversation, and how he finally sort of walked us around to concluding that his partner had stolen the money and taken off."

"It wasn't until we learned about Mr. Meredith's gambling habit that we became suspicious," Smith said. His first substantive contribution to the conversation.

"Yeah, I understand Meredith was into someone in Vegas for several hundred thousand dollars," I said.

"He was, and not just *someone* either. He owed Vinnie 'The Shark' D'Angelo. Vinnie's one of the old mob hangers-on from the old days of Vegas. He's suspected of at least a half dozen . . . disappearances of people who'd crossed him."

"Then, Meredith supposedly paid Vinnie what he owed him," Smith said. "Sometime in October, but we were unable to nail down the specific date."

"Shit, that would make Meredith the prime suspect in my book," I said.

"It does in mine, too," she said, and Smith nodded. "But, unless we can find Whelan and get his side of the story, it's just supposition. Not enough to take to a U.S. Attorney. Even the SAIC's beginning to think we're wasting time on it. So, if you could get us something, anything, it'd be great."

"I'll give it my best shot."

"You'll keep this between us?" she said.

"Mum's the word," I said. "It's like the seal of the confessional, what you tell me stays with me."

"It's important that Meredith not get wind that we suspect him of anything," Smith said.

"I know how to be discrete. Besides, since I'm already working for him, I've got a free pass to snoop around and ask him questions."

That seemed to placate Smith—a little. Wentworth just smiled at me.

We shook hands and they left. I now had official FBI blessing to dig into Meredith's stuff. All I had to do was find his partner. Do I get strange cases, or what? First, I'm hired to find a woman who is dead, and now, the FBI wants me to find a guy who has run away and disappeared into thin air.

Piece of cake.

Charles Ray

# THIRTEEN

As soon as the two FBI agents were out the door, I called Heather into my office. I know I told Wentworth and Smith that I'd keep it to myself, but Heather and I are partners. We're a package deal. You hire one of us, you get both of us. Besides, I needed her to get information I'd need to work Meredith.

"Our problem is now officially solved," I said. "The feds want me to investigate Meredith. So, I'll keep looking for his wife, knowing she's dead, and I'll never find her, while at the same time, looking into his business on behalf of Uncle Sam."

Her eyebrows arched upward. "Which means the FBI ran into a brick wall, and they want us to do their jobs for them."

"Of course, but who cares?" I explained

the situation. As usual, she was quick on the uptake.

"So, they want us to find Whelan," she said. "If they can't find him with all their access to sophisticated surveillance, how do they expect us to do it?"

"I thought about that," I said. "I'm thinking the way to find Whelan is through Meredith, and since I'm already working for him, I have access. If the FBI starts poking around him, he's liable to spook and take a powder. Anyway, maybe the way to find Whelan is to start with the last time we know they were together, and track Meredith's movements from that point."

"You think maybe Meredith did something to his partner?"

Like I said, she's quick on the uptake. That idea had come to me near the end of my conversation with Wentworth and Smith. If Whelan had disappeared at the same time as a substantial sum of money, and it just so happened that Meredith owed a large sum to a mobster, it was within the realm of possibility that Meredith stole the money to pay his debt, and then threw suspicion on his missing partner. The question was, how did Meredith make Whelan disappear? Tracking Meredith's movements might just give us a clue.

"Yeah, I think he just might have. The challenge's going to be proving it, so get started with tracking everything Meredith did and everywhere he went from say, October 7 to date."

"And, what will you be doing while I'm doing that?"

"I'll be doing what I do best," I said. "I'll be kicking over rocks and see what crawls out."

I left her at her computer and went into my office. I hadn't started my notebook on the case, other than a few scribbles in my pocket notebook, so I pulled a fresh one from my desk drawer and opened it to the first page.

Heather likes to give our cases names. She says it's for when she finally convinces me to write a book or two about our adventures—the names will help us come up with titles. That ain't gonna happen, but having a name for the case does do one thing; it helps me focus on the essentials. So, I spent a few minutes coming up with a good name. Finally, I hit on, The Case of the Missing Wife. Not the most original name, but I liked it.

I wrote it in big block letters at the top of the first page. Then, I drew a line down the center of the page. On the left side, I wrote, CAROLINE MEREDITH – MISSING OR DEAD, and on the right I wrote, NOAH WHELAN – DEAD OR MISSING. I thought that was pretty cute.

Then, I wrote down everything I knew about both situations. Under Caroline's name, I wrote:

*Auto Accident?*
*ID'ed by Father*
*Cremated – why?*
*Abused by husband?*
*Did family know? – talk to Sheldon Logan!*

Under Whelan's, I wrote the following:

*Argument with Meredith about money*
*Disappeared shortly after argument*

Not a lot to go on in either case, but it helped me see where I needed to focus my information-gathering effort. As much as it pained me, I was going to have to take another run at Matt Donahue. If his daughter was being abused, he should have had some suspicions. At a distance, without the man's war record to cloud my judgment, I could see that he'd been withholding something from me. I'd have to put my feelings aside and find out what that was. First, though, I needed to talk to Logan. My gut was telling me that if anyone knew what was going on in Caroline's life, it would be him.

Once I got that out of the way, I was going to go after the Whelan case. Then, I got a brain flash. I pulled out my cell phone and dialed Aaron Cooper's number. He answered on the first ring.

"You said you saw Whelan and Meredith arguing over money," I said. "Do you remember the date of that argument?"

"Yeah," he said. "It was the 7th or 8th of October."

I appended that information to the first item under Whelan's name.

Charles Ray

# FOURTEEN

Damascus, Maryland is an unincorporated town with a population of around 11,000, located near Maryland Routes 27 and 108. It's in affluent Montgomery County, near the Patuxent River and the border with rural Howard County, and is surrounded by family-owned farms.

Castle Creek Hospital, at the intersection of Main Street and Woodfield Road, was in fact just a large clinic with about ten beds for inpatients. The parking lot was twice the area of the building itself, but nearly filled with pickups and older model cars. I found a space in the farthest corner from the building itself, and hiked back to reception, where a heavyweight redhead behind the desk told me to have a seat in the waiting area, and that

Dr. Logan would be with me as soon as he finished with the patient he was seeing.

The waiting area spanned most of the front of the building not taken up by the reception desk. Straight backed plastic benches wide enough for four people each were scattered about with plastic cubes containing outdated copies of magazines no wanted to read. There were twenty people scattered about, either waiting to see a doctor or waiting for someone who was being seen by a doctor. I didn't see any bleeding sores, nor was anyone hacking up their lungs, so I didn't get the creepy feelings I usually get whenever I enter a hospital. I found a bench that was unoccupied, and far enough away from the other waiters to make me feel less uncomfortable, and sat down slantwise to discourage anyone from joining me.

My butt and thighs were beginning to ache from the hard plastic, which was also felt several degrees cooler than the air, when a tall, skinny guy wearing green scrubs under a white jacket came from the back and walked over to the reception desk, scanning the waiting area as he walked. The woman at the desk pointed in my direction, and he came over.

"I'm Sheldon Logan. You wanted to talk to me?" he asked. There was a hint of the deep south in his accent.

I showed him my ID. "I'm looking into your cousin's accident," I said. "You mind if I ask you a few questions?"

He looked long and hard, first at my ID, and then at me.

"Why does a private eye want to investigate my cousin's accident? The police already did that, and they've issued their report."

His expression was one of deep suspicion, and his tone was almost belligerent. With him, I decided that my usual play of letting the interviewee make assumptions, usually wrong, and see where things went.

"I know," I said. "But, there are a few things about it that . . . don't really add up. I've been hired to take a second look."

If he asked who hired me I was in trouble. I'd either have to lie, or tell the truth and risk him shutting down. I was lucky, though. He made an assumption.

"It's the insurance company, right? They don't want to pay the claim."

I had him, but I didn't want to take it too far, just in case he got it into his head to call the insurance company and complain. Hell, I didn't even know which insurance company insured the car Caroline was driving.

"No, it's not that," I said. "It's really just a matter of filling in all the blanks, you know."

"What blanks? The damn car skidded on the ice and hit a pole, and Caroline was killed, what more do you need to know?"

"Well, for one thing, what was her state of mind in the days before the accident? Was she depressed or upset in any way?"

Now, the look of suspicion was replaced by one of anger. His face turned the color of nearly ripe tomatoes and a little 'v' formed between his eyebrows.

"What the hell? Are you trying to insinuate that she might have crashed on purpose?" He sprayed spittle as he talked, and his voice rose at the end.

I held a hand up to calm him down. "No, no, that's not what I'm saying at all." Then, I decided to take a slightly different approach. "Look, we heard rumors, unsubstantiated, you understand, that Ms. Meredith and her husband were having problems . . . that maybe there was . . . some abuse in the household. I don't want to bring a subject like this up with her father, and you'll understand how difficult it would be to talk to the husband about it. I sort of figured . . . well, you and she were close, and I thought if there were problems, she might have shared them with you."

That pulled him up short. He still looked a little miffed, but I could see from the way his eyes darted from side to side, he was cooking up something in that mind of his.

"Well . . . I can't say for sure, you understand," he finally said. "But, Caroline was a bit put out the week before the accident. Sort of distracted, you know, and that slug of a husband of hers is certainly capable of abuse."

Pretty slick. He didn't come right out and accuse Meredith of abuse, but he really planted the seed.

"So, you never saw bruises, or any other signs of abuse? What about verbal abuse? That's usually a precursor to physical abuse. When you saw them together, was he ever verbally abusive?"

"To tell you the truth, except for the wedding, I never saw them together. I'd meet Caroline from time to time at her father's house over in Germantown, but Matt and Jackson get along like a mangy dog and a feral cat, so Jackson never came with her. Say, you're not thinking he might have done something to her, are you?"

I looked around. While no one was obviously eavesdropping, I did notice that a few heads seemed to be inclined in our direction.

"Look, is there some place private where we can continue this conversation?"

"I have a cramped office in back, if you don't mind," he said.

I followed him through the waiting room to a door marked EXAMINATION ROOMS, and down a short hallway to a door at the end. He hadn't exaggerated when he called it cramped. It had a small desk with an extension arm upon which rested a laptop, a small armless swivel chair behind the desk, and a straight back chair beside the desk opposite the computer. The top of the desk was covered with large green folders and even larger cardboard sleeves containing X-rays. An X-ray screen took up the wall to his left, and an eye chart the wall on the right. The wall behind his desk was covered in color illustrations of the human body—mostly the inside. His medical school diploma hung on the wall just to the left of the door. That wall was otherwise blank. He motioned me to the straight back chair.

"To answer your question," I said when he was seated. "It's unlikely her husband could have had anything to do with her accident. He was out of the country at the time. In Hong Kong, I believe."

"True, but Jackson Meredith is not without influence and connections. He could have hired someone to, say, tamper with her car or something."

"The police checked the car, and didn't find anything wrong with it."

"Then, it was just an unfortunate accident. Case closed."

I was losing him. I had to get him back to Meredith. There was more, I just knew it. Call it intuition, or call it gut feeling, but something about Sheldon Logan wasn't adding up. In the first place, the only emotion he'd shown so far was anger when he thought I was suggesting his cousin might have deliberately driven her car into that pole. What was missing was any sign of grief. If Sheldon was as close to Caroline as Matt

Donahue had told me, there should be signs of grief, of loss. Now that I was noticing that lack in him, it occurred to me that it had been missing in Donahue as well. He had only shown emotion when talking about his son-in-law.

Funny how your mind makes connections when you least expect it. I'd been so focused on Donahue's military status I'd neglected to pay close attention to his body language. Thankfully, the mind never really forgets what the eyes see. It just stores it away until some stimulus triggers the memory. Logan's lack of grief had brought back what I'd seen, or not seen, in Donahue.

One more puzzle. What were they hiding, and what did it have to do with Caroline Meredith's accident?

Charles Ray

# FIFTEEN

After leaving Logan in his office and making my way back to my car, I sat in it, letting the engine run to warm up the interior. While I waited, I called Heather to tell her I was stopping by Jackson Meredith's place of business before returning to the office.

From Damascus I took Route 108 to the rural town of Olney and got on Georgia Avenue for the drive south to the I-495 Washington Beltway. East on the Beltway to Route 1 was a nightmare due to an eighteen-wheeler side swiping a cement truck near the New Hampshire Avenue off ramp, blocking traffic for forty minutes. Ninety minutes after leaving Damascus, I exited I-495 on US 1 south, driving through College Park and Hyattsville, which look less like towns than suburban shopping strips, toward the District line. WheMer Developers was a two story industrial looking combination office-warehouse complex on the right. I parked in one of the ten visitor slots and made my way to the main entrance.

I entered a high-ceilinged space with glass topped tables and futuristic looking chairs on the left arranged in little conversation groups, and a stainless steel curved desk on the right behind which sat a fashion-model thin blonde with big boobs that were straining to burst out of her scoop-necked blouse.

"Hi, can I help you?" she asked.

"I need to speak with Jackson Meredith," I said.

"Do you have an appointment?"

I took my ID out and laid it on the desk. She hardly even looked down at it.

"I'm a private investigator, hired by Jackson Meredith, and I'm here to discuss that investigation with him," I said. "So, if you'd kindly let him know I'm here, I'd really appreciate it."

"I'm sorry, sir, but Mr. Meredith doesn't see anyone without an appointment."

I leaned forward until my face was less than a foot from hers, causing her to scoot her wheeled chair backwards.

"Listen, young lady," I said. "I'm a busy man, and I don't have time for messing around." I put my most menacing growl in my voice and glared down at her until the only color left on her face was her too-red lipstick. "Now, you get on the phone, or intercom, or use smoke signals if you have to, but you let Meredith know I'm here to see him."

Her hand trembled like a willow tree in a stiff breeze as she picked the phone up and stuttered something unintelligible into it. As she listened, her eyes got round. When she hung up, she looked up at me, still pale, and with trembling lips.

"M-mister M-meredith's secretary will b-be out to escort you m-momentarily," she said. Tears formed in the corner of her eyes.

I turned and walked to the nearest chair and sat with my back to her. The reading material on the small side tables, *National Geographic, Cosmopolitan, Sports Illustrated,* and *The New Yorker* was several notches above the hospital in Damascus. I was ten pages into the latest issue of *National Geographic,* reading about a lost city that had been discovered in some desert in the Middle East, when a shadow fell over me.

I looked up to see a middle aged woman with iron gray hair done up in a severe bun, wearing a dress that went out of style with the Beetles, and an expression as severe as her hairstyle.

"You're Mr. Pennyback?" she asked.

I looked around. There were no other visitors waiting, so who else would I be. So far, the staff of WheMer didn't impress me.

"Yes, I am," I said.

"Please follow me." She spun on her heel and walked away without looking back.

I followed.

We walked around the faux wall behind the receptionist. I hadn't noticed it before. The corridor behind the wall wound to the left in a slight serpentine pattern, with doors on each side, offset from each other, so that the occupants of one office couldn't see in the other even if both doors were open. At the end of the corridor, we entered a large elevator, which shot silently to the second floor.

The space we entered on the second floor was regal looking, a sharp contrast to the spaceship décor on the first floor. Deep purple plush carpeting covered the floor. The reception area in front of the elevator was smaller than downstairs, too, with only four chairs around a kidney-shaped table. Another middle aged woman, with brown hair cut in a page boy, sat behind the reception desk. She looked up and smiled as we breezed past and into a straightedge-straight hallway with four doors, two on each side.

My guide, who hadn't bothered to tell me her name, marched stiffly to the second door on the right and rapped lightly. I heard a muffled voice. She opened the door and stood aside.

"You may go in," she said.

The area outside Meredith's office was

plush. Inside his office it was over the top. Walking across the dark green carpet from the door felt like walking on a thick carpet of moss. The walls were covered in velveteen fabric, a dust-red color, and were covered with photos of Meredith with various movers and shakers around the Washington area, including a couple of senators and a Supreme Court justice, and with certificates from various civic organizations from the District, Maryland, Virginia, New Jersey, and Pennsylvania. His desk was four feet deep and six feet wide, dark mahogany with intricate carvings at the corner. The chair he sat in had a high black leather back and thick leather-covered arm rests. His in and out boxes were silver, and from the sheen, I doubted that was just the color. He sat in his chair like some ancient potentate granting an audience to one of his peasants, staring at me with piggy eyes and a feral grin on his face.

He waved a hand imperiously, indicating that I should take a seat in a large straight back chair with padded arm rests that sat in front of his desk and slightly offset to the right. This guy was full of himself. His 'I love me' wall beat the worst I'd seen in the Pentagon where some of the generals almost make a religion out of their own image, and to top it off, the way he'd placed the visitor's chair indicated that he liked to play mind games. He had it in a position that established his dominance over whoever occupied it.

I decided to play along for a bit, but he was in for a surprise. Just like the coral snake, which is one of the smaller poisonous snakes in East Texas where I grew up, when I sink my teeth in, I don't let go, and I pack a wallop.

I sat and looked levelly at him. I knew he was waiting for me to say something. I'd come to him, and as the 'supplicant,' it was on me to begin. I remained silent until he began to look uncomfortable.

When I learned meditation, one of the things my teacher taught me that can really freak some people out when they see it, is how to keep my eyes open, without blinking, for as long as five minutes. Having someone sit looking, without blinking their eyes, starts to freak most people out around the thirty second mark. To his credit, Meredith made it to fifty seconds before he blinked.

"Uh, okay, Pennyback," he said. "What do you have for me.?"

If you want to establish control of a conversation, you have to set the pace. That means not responding immediately to a question. I looked at him, silently counting, one-Mississippi, two-Mississippi, three-Mississippi, four-Mississippi, five-Mississippi, before answering him.

"Like we told you when you signed the contract, there are no guarantees. We're still looking into this."

I could tell it was getting to him, and that he knew what I was doing, and it pissed him to have his own techniques turned against him.

"Don't you have anything, some idea where my wife's hiding?"

Interesting that he'd use that word—hiding. Why would he think his wife would be 'hiding' from him?

"What I've found so far indicates your wife *was* killed in that auto accident. The police reports were quite thorough, and her father identified the body."

His face turned red. A muscle under his left eye twitched.

"I don't give a fuck what the police reports say, and as for Matt Donahue, that fucker hates me. I know he's helping Caroline hide from me."

I realized then that he had poor impulse control, a characteristic of many bullies. When angry, he was likely to blurt out things, as he did the word 'hiding,' without thinking. The trick would be to get him just angry enough, without giving away what information I was interested in.

I leaned forward in a semi-aggressive posture and stared directly into his eyes.

"Why would your wife want to hide from you?"

Now, a muscle under his right eye was twitching. He eased his chair back a fraction of an inch, ceding ground to me.

"Uh, she wouldn't," he said. "I didn't mean she was hiding from me . . . I meant that son of a bitch of a father of hers was keeping her from me."

`    I decided to press my advantage.

"Same question—why would your wife's father want to hide her from you? Could it be that he thinks you're in some way a threat to her?"

His eyes went from round like tiny saucers to narrow slits in a fraction of a second. I could tell I was getting to him. His body was nearly vibrating.

"What the fuck do you mean by that question?"

He glared at me, a look that I'm sure he'd used with good effect on many of his employees. It didn't work on me. I glared right back.

"Let's just say that I've come into possession of some information that indicates all was not necessarily lovey-dovey between you and your wife. Also, that maybe you have a tendency to express your displeasure in, shall we say, physical terms."

The guy might be filthy rich, but he wasn't all that smart. It took him a while to process what I'd just said. When he did, his look got angrier.

"Who do you think you are, accusing me of . . . what . . . beating my wife? I never laid a finger on her. Did that shit heel of a father of hers tell you that?"

He sprayed spittle all over his nice clean desk. I wasn't done with him, though, not by a long shot.

"There are ways of being abusive that don't involve actually hitting someone," I said.

"Like what, for instance?"

Talk about stupid. Most people would have immediately thought of verbal abuse or bullying. I decided to move down another path to see how he reacted.

"I also heard that you have a tendency to be abusive with your employees and co-workers."

"That's a crock of shit," he said. "Who told you that?"

"Doesn't matter who told me. You clearly have anger issues, Meredith, and you take things out on other people—your former partner, for instance."

I was watching him closely as I said that, and I caught the momentary flicker of fear in his eyes. His partner, ex-partner, was clearly a sore subject.

"Hey, until stole five million from our cash account and took off, we got along well." He looked away from me as he spoke. A sign of deception.

"Is that so? I hear the two of you had a knock-down, drag-out argument just before he disappeared."

He fought it, but the look of nervousness

was there for a moment. He was more concerned over questions about his former partner than he'd been at my insinuation that he beat his wife. His mouth opened and closed, but he said nothing. He just sat there, staring at me.

"Would that argument have had anything to do with money, by any chance? Maybe related to your little gambling problem and the money you owed some Vegas mobster?"

He exploded out of his chair, leaned over the desk and waved his fist in my face.

"You . . . what . . . you been investigating me? How dare you! I hired you to find my wife, not snoop into my affairs."

I noticed he didn't bother denying anything I'd said.

"I'm thorough," I said. "When my partner and I take a case, we look into everything about everyone involved."

I didn't even move away from his fist. Instead, I stared right into his bloodshot eyes. He got the message, and sat back down, straightening his jacket and trying to compose his expression. Finally, he sighed.

"Okay," he said. "So I like to gamble, and like most gamblers, I lose more than I win. But, I paid my markers, so I'm free and clear on that." He hesitated, looking at a point a foot to the right of my face rather than directly at me. "And, yeah, me and Noah had an argument, but it was about some cost overruns on a project. I wanted to spend a little extra to make it really first class, but he was always pinching pennies. I couldn't believe it when he nearly cleaned us out and took off."

He kept hitting on that. That was what he wanted me to focus on, and I was, only not quite the way he wanted. There was something going on concerning his missing partner, and a little voice in the back of my mind was telling me that it wasn't anything good.

Charles Ray

# SIXTEEN

I went back to the office and shared my day with Heather. She made copious notes to put in the computerized case file. I went into my office and called Agent Wentworth.

When she came on, I told her I'd talked to Meredith about his missing partner.

"Uh, I wish you'd checked with me before you did that, Pennyback," she said. "You could blow our case."

"Don't worry, it just came up in the course of a conversation we had about the case he hired me for. Nothing was said about an FBI investigation, or even that anyone suspected he might have helped his partner . . . disappear."

There was a long pause.

"What do you mean by that?" she asked

finally.

I explained how Meredith reacted when I switched subjects to his partner.

"How confident are you in your ability to correctly interpret body language?" she asked.

"Pretty damn confident. It saved my life more than a time or two when I was in the army."

"Damn, you know what that means."

Yeah, I knew what it meant, had known almost from the moment Meredith had spooked when I mentioned his partner's name, and how fear had crossed his face the longer I talked.

"It means you're now working a possible . . . no, strike 'possible' . . . this *is* a murder case," I said.

I heard her exhale.

"I don't know how you can be so sure," she said. "But, you and I have come to the same conclusion. The problem is, we have no hard evidence . . . no body, and the U.S. Attorney we're working with on this case is a stickler for such things. Mention gut feelings or hunches to him and he laughs you out of his office."

"I know what you mean," I said. "It's a pain in the ass, but he does have a point. You can't get a conviction without solid evidence."

"So, Al Pennyback, the ball's in your court. You have to get us some evidence to nail this bastard. I know it'll be like finding a needle in a haystack, but I have a feeling if anyone can do it, you can."

I laughed. "It'll be like finding a needle in a stack of needles, but, this guy's a bully and a murderer. He can't be allowed to get away with it. I'll find you your evidence."

"Just be careful," she said. "If he did murder his partner, chances are he wouldn't hesitate to come after you."

"I know that, but he wouldn't be the first to try." I've been in a bad guy's crosshairs more times than I care to count. Meredith didn't begin to measure up to enemies I'd faced in my life. "I'm almost wishing he'll try."

"Hey, Kemo Sabe," she said. "We want to take him alive. Wouldn't do for you to put a bullet in him, even if it would save the government the cost of a trial."

"You don't have to worry about that. I don't even own a gun. I figure if I can't fight my way out of a situation with my fists, I can always run like hell."

She laughed. I liked the sound of her laughter.

"Al Pennyback," she said. "You are a strange man."

If she only knew.

Charles Ray

# SEVENTEEN

I woke up early on Saturday morning, roused Sandra out of bed, exercised, meditated, showered, and cooked breakfast. After breakfast, I called Carlton Raine to ask if I could drop by his place for a visit. Of course, he said come out right away for late breakfast, and sounded disappointed when I informed him we'd already eaten. So, we compromised. Sandra and I would join him and Elizabeth for lunch.

The temperature, chilly during our run, had risen to a comfortable level by the time we pulled on our coats and crammed into my Volkswagen for the drive to Raine's place. Saturday morning traffic, mostly a few fans and SUVs filled with families taking advantage of the brisk fall weather for trips to

the countryside, was light. By the time we
arrived at the turnoff onto the dirt road
leading to his cabin, we were the only vehicle
on the road.

Calling the path to Raine's house was
being generous. It was hardly more than tire
tracks in the brown grass that wound snake-
like between two barbed wire fences; four
strands of razor wire strung on six-foot high
wooden poles. The only indication that
anyone lived down the path was a discrete
white sign at the turnoff that read, PRIVATE
PROPERTY – NO TRESPASSING. NO
HUNTING. VIOLATERS WILL BE
PROSECUTED. That was new, installed after
Raine was forced to chase two deer hunters
off the year before.

The Volkswagen's tires made crunching
sounds on the hard packed dirt of the trail as
we drove slowly toward our destination.

The one-story solidly built log cabin came
into view as we made the last serpentine
turn, hunkered down in the center of an area
over a hundred and fifty meters in diameter
that was cleared of all vegetation in every
direction, with close-cropped grass. Off to the
left of the cabin was a wooden shed in which
Raine kept his Toyota 4-Runner and the
Chevy Camaro belonging to Elizabeth Sung,
who had moved from her Chinatown
apartment and taken up permanent
residence with him.

He waited until we'd parked and got out

before waving at us. A broad smile creased his nut brown face. His hair, close cropped in military style, was now completely white, but that and a few lines on his face were the only signs of his eighty-plus years. His dark brown eyes were clear and his posture was erect, and he still looked like someone you wouldn't want to tussle with.

When we mounted the steps, he stepped forward and kissed Sandra on the cheek and then shook my hand.

"Welcome, you two," he said in that slight southern accent of his. "It's been a while since I had the pleasure of your company." That last was aimed at Sandra, not at me.

He led us into the large living room and motioned at the big sofa that sat facing the door, pushing the steel reinforced door shut with his shoulder.

"Elizabeth's in the kitchen putting the finishing touches on lunch," he said. "Would you two like a pre-dinner libation while we wait?"

"Nothing for me," Sandra said, taking off her jacket and tossing it over the arm of the sofa. "I think I'll go out to the kitchen and help Liz."

We watched her go. After she passed through the door leading to the kitchen, Raine picked up her jacket and hung it on a rack near the door. I took mine off and hung it next to hers.

"How about you, youngster," he said. "I've

got a bottle of Wild Turkey bourbon that I've been saving for a special occasion."

"I wouldn't say no, but is this really a special occasion?"

He looked meaningfully toward the kitchen. "Of course it is," he said. "Elizabeth and I discussed it before you got here. You come so seldom, whenever you do, it's a special occasion for me."

"In other words, she won't let you open it and drink alone."

"Well, that too," he said. "You want some or not?"

He had an almost pleading look on his face. I laughed. "Put that way, how can I refuse? I'll take mine neat."

He walked to the large cabinet near the metal door leading to his backroom command post, opened it and withdrew a large bottle of amber liquor. "Is there any other way?" He half-filled two 8-ounce Old Fashioned glasses and handed me one. "Over the lips and past the gums, look out stomach, here it comes," he said and took a long pull.

I took a sip. I hadn't had bourbon for a while, and the woody liquid burned my tongue at first. The second sip, though, was smooth, and by the third, my taste buds were welcoming the warmth.

He led me back to the sofa. He sat at one end, and motioned me to the other.

"I guess you know I'm here because I need some of your sage advice," I said.

Ever since Quincy Chang introduced me to Carlton Raine a few years back when I was working on a case involving a Chinese gangster who wanted me dead, he'd become something of a mentor. One of the first blacks to be hired by the agency as a field agent, he was something of a legend in the intelligence and special operations community. His nickname was 'Blood,' and not from the old slang term for black men. He still had connections with some of the old hands at Langley, who let him have some of their new toys to evaluate before sending them out to the field. On one or two occasions, he'd let me 'borrow' them.

He took another sip, smaller this time.

"Doesn't matter why you're here, Al, you know I just like having you visit from time to time."

I used to think he said that because he was lonely, but since Elizabeth, who he'd had a hand in rescuing from that same Chinese gangster I mentioned, had moved in with him, that no longer seemed the case. I was beginning to think he actually liked having me around because I was good company—or, that because I'd been in army special ops, he liked having someone around who understood what he'd gone through. Whatever the reason, I liked his company too.

"So," he said. "What's the puzzle this time?"

If Daisy Wentworth knew I was sharing

information with him, she'd probably have a fit. And, I understood her position. If word of what I was doing got to Meredith, it could totally tank the FBI's investigation, and now that it looked like a murder case, and not just theft or embezzlement, it was even more critical that it succeed. But, I trusted Blood Raine with my life. If there was anyone I knew who could keep a secret, it was a man whose entire adult life had been spent in the world of intelligence, where even your identity is sometimes kept secret from the people you associate with. I told him everything.

While I talked, he sipped, and when I stopped, his glass was empty. I'd finished about half mine, so he stood, took my glass and went back to the cabinet and refilled both glasses to the three-quarter mark this time. I winced—Sandra would be driving us home.

After taking his seat, he put his glass on the end table and turned to face me. "This Meredith fellow sounds like a real piece of work," he said. "Do you think he stole the money from the company, and then killed his partner and threw the blame on him?"

I followed his lead and put my glass on the end table at my end of the sofa, hoping he wouldn't notice. Fat chance, he frowned at me, but said nothing.

"It's the only thing that makes sense," I said. "The FBI found no trace of the partner in Miami, and with the resources they have it's unlikely he'd be able to totally escape their notice. No, the only thing that makes sense is that Meredith killed him and hid the body somewhere. The problem is, though, without a body the FBI doesn't have much of a case."

"So, you'll just have to find it for them, son."

"That's easier said than done, Blood. Do you know how many places there are in the Washington metro area where you could stash a corpse that might never be found?"

"A lot," he said. Of course, he'd know such things. "But, a guy like Meredith is likely to use a place he's familiar with."

"You've got a point. If I could find out who got on that plane here in Washington pretending to be Noah Whelan, maybe I could get a lead."

"You're barking up the wrong tree." He shook his head. "I doubt he'd let anyone else know what he did. Chances are he hired someone to do that and told him it to play a joke on someone. I doubt he'd tell him he killed someone. No, if you want to catch a fox, you have to think like a fox. Now, if you were Meredith, and you wanted to make a body disappear, where would you put it?"

I thought about everything I'd heard or learned since I started working on the case— and then, it hit me. "Aaron Cooper, the guy Meredith fired," I said. "He said Meredith wanted to pour the concrete early on a project they were working on in . . . Mount Airy. I don't know why that didn't occur to me right away. If you want to hide a body, what better place than under a few tons of shopping center."

"Now you're using that brain of yours."

I frowned. "But, if the concrete's already poured, we're sunk. I doubt the FBI would be able to get a warrant to bust up a construction project just on my hunch. Hell, I doubt they'd even try."

"Well then, you'll just have to get Meredith to confess."

I was astonished. That had to be the craziest . . . then, on the other hand, given Meredith's inability to control his anger, if I played it right, I just might.

"It won't be easy," I said. "But, it might work."

"Well, that's one problem solved," he said.

"What do you mean? That was my only problem."

"Not really, son. You still have to find Caroline Meredith."

"But, she's dead. Her dad identified the body. I have no idea why Meredith hired me to find her, but that was, if you'll pardon a sick play on words, was a dead end from the start."

He waggled a finger at me.

"Al, you weren't listening to yourself," he said. "You said both the father and the cousin seemed unaffected by this woman's death, right?"

"Yeah, but the old man's a war veteran, and the cousin's a doctor, both accustomed to dealing with death. Maybe that's just their way of coping."

"Hell fire, son, you don't believe that any more than I do. I don't care how much war you've seen, the loss of a child will hit you where it hurts. Their reactions were not natural, and you sensed it, you just don't want to admit it for some reason. Son, if it walks like a duck, looks like a duck, and quacks like a duck, it's a dang duck."

He was right, of course. My rational brain had been telling me that all along, but its voice was overridden by my reaction to Donahue's war veteran status.

"Okay, so after I help the FBI put Meredith away, I'll put the screws to Donahue and Logan and get them to tell me where Caroline is. Hell, if he's in jail, they might just come forward without me having to do anything."

"Don't count on that," he said. "You're forgetting one thing."

"What's that?"

"Where did they get the body the father identified? Someone died. You just might be looking at another murder."

Shit, I hadn't thought about that.

Charles Ray

# EIGHTEEN

Raine hadn't overlooked my still-full glass of bourbon, and he insisted we finish it. By the time lunch was served, I had a good buzz on, and a glass of wine with the breaded pork chops and stir fried *bak choi* left me unable to drive home. Raine and Elizabeth were into their own strange brand of fusion cuisine, combining southern and Chinese food, but it was great. I woke up on Sunday with a hangover, my first in years, so Sandra and I skipped exercise, had dry toast and coffee for breakfast and spent the day in bed.

On Monday, Thanksgiving week, I got to the office early, only five minutes behind Heather. I filled her in on my conversation with Raine and my plan to get a confession out of Meredith.

"I know you can be pretty persuasive," she said. "But, are you sure you're up to this?"

"The guy's got a hair trigger temper. All I have to do is push him in the right direction, I'm pretty sure his mouth will do the rest."

"Yes, but don't forget, when his partner confronted him, he killed him."

"Well, there is that," I said. "But, I've gone up against better than him. I think I can handle it. My *real* problem's gonna be the Caroline Meredith situation after this piece of shit's behind bars."

She looked confused, so I explained Raine's conclusion about Donahue, and possibly the cousin as well.

"I can't believe it," she said. Her expression was one of shock. "From your description of Mr. Donahue, he seems like a decent man. That just doesn't sound like something he'd do."

"I know. I find it hard to believe myself. But, if Caroline Meredith *is* still alive, I feel obligated to find out who did die to cover her disappearance." She looked like she wanted to cry. Hell, I felt like I wanted to cry. "We'll deal with that later. For now, call Cooper and tell him I'm on my way, and to dress warmly."

"Why? What if he asks why?"

"Tell him I'll tell him when I get there."

Monday morning traffic driving across the District was like a demolition derby. I saw five fender benders before getting to Dupont Circle. My mood was anything but rosy as I rang Cooper's doorbell. Cooper must have been waiting for me. He opened the door before the sound of the bell died.

"Come on in," he said. "I was just fixing myself a cup of chamomile tea, would you like one?"

"No, thanks, I'd really like to get going if you don't mind."

He looked flustered. "Yeah, your, er, associate said for me to wear a warm coat. Where is it you want to go?"

"I want you to show me that shopping mall construction project you were talking about when I was here last," I said.

"Whoa! I'm not going out there. That shit Meredith's likely to be there, and I have no desire to see or be seen by him any time soon."

"Don't worry about that. I just need you to show me where the place is. I doubt Meredith will even be there."

He didn't look convinced, but I outweighed him by probably fifty pounds and he had to crane his neck to look up at me. It was the devil in his face versus the potential of the devil that I suspected Meredith could be. The devil in his face won.

He donned a dark blue hooded North Face down jacket and followed me out to my car.

From his house we drove to Connecticut Avenue, and then north through Bethesda's central business district to I-495. We took the Beltway west to the beginning of I-270 where, thankfully, the northbound traffic was relatively light, and drove north on I-270 to State Route 27 just north of Germantown. Route 27 is a mostly two-lane highway that winds through parklands and farms, slicing through the center of Damascus, crosses the Patuxent River at one of its narrowest points, dives under I-70, and goes through Mount Airy on its way to Pennsylvania.

Located in hilly country at the headwaters of the Patapsco River west of Baltimore, Mount Airy is a small town that was built in the 1800s to accommodate the east-west railroad. With the demise of rail traffic, most of the population of the town, which straddles Carroll and Frederick counties, commute to either Baltimore or the DC area to work. Called the 'Four Counties Area' by locals, the surrounding farmlands are located in Carroll, Frederick, Montgomery, and Howard Counties.

Entering the town proper, Route 27 becomes Main Street, a two-lane thoroughfare flanked by turn of the century style red brick or wood frame buildings, with many of the two-story buildings having wrap-around second floor galleries with wooden railings, giving it the appearance of the small towns in movies from the 1940s and 50s.

The construction project was near the Mount Airy Carnival Grounds on Ridge Road, a two-lane street that ran northeast off Main Street. It was recognizable from several blocks away from the tall, yellow crane squatting amidst several dump trucks, a cement mixer, and five pickup trucks, around which hard-hatted workers scurried like ants.

To my untrained eye, it wasn't a shopping mall—not yet. The area, about one city block on each side, was a large area of disturbed earth with a rectangular area in the middle that was about thirty feet deep and a hundred feet long, with six tall concrete pylons jutting up from the reddish-brown earth. Starting at the left side, they were in rows of three, front to back along the short side of the rectangle, and ending about two-thirds of the way along the long side. The final third of the rectangle was a rough concrete pad. From the shape and size of the rectangle, I imagined this would be a small strip mall with six or eight businesses, unless there were plans to include other businesses in the lot, which dwarfed what construction I could see.

I parked the Volkswagen on the street and got out.

"I'll wait in the car if you don't mind," Cooper said just before I closed the door.

I looked over at the workers, a few of whom had stopped what they were doing and were standing looking at us. A pot-bellied man, with his dirty blue shirt drooping out over his jeans, and wearing a white hard hat, walked toward us. He didn't look friendly.

He stopped five feet away and put his hands on his hips. He looked from me to Cooper who had hunched down in the seat.

"Something I can do for you, mister?" he asked.

I debated whether to be up front or run a con on him—for a fraction of a second—then, decided this guy was just a working stiff who had no skin in Meredith's game, so I fished out my ID and held it up so he could see it.

"I was hired to look into some things related to the company, and I'm just here to look around and ask a few questions," I said. "I take it you're the supervisor?"

"Yeah, Mike Wozniak," he said. He pulled off a glove and shoved a grimy hand at me. "What kinda questions you got?"

This was where I had to tread carefully. My goal was to get as much information from him as possible without raising his suspicions, and giving him cause to go to Meredith. I wanted my confrontation with my client to be on my terms.

"I understand you had a little work stoppage on this project not too long ago," I said.

He grimaced, an open-mouth twisting downward of his chapped lips, revealing tobacco-stained teeth.

"Yeah, that shi-, uh, Mr. Meredith come out here and ordered us to start pouring concrete for the foundation floor before we'd put in the load-bearing columns. I refused, and he threatened to tear up our contract. Well, I told him what for and walked my boys off the site."

I looked over his shoulder at the partial floor at the right end of the site.

"Looks like he got it partially done," I said.

"Oh that, yeah, he . . . Meredith . . . hired some scabs, a bunch of Salvadorians, to come out and start pouring. I got wind of it, and went to the union and they musta called him and threatened a lawsuit, 'cause right after they poured that, they were pulled off. Meredith himself called and apologized and asked if we'd come back to work. He even offered to pay us for the four days we were on strike and throw in a little bonus to boot. Said, he'd been out of line and he'd make it up to us."

"So, what do you plan to do about the part that's already poured? Won't that make it difficult to put the columns in place?"

"Sure as hell will," he said. "I offered to rip it out and re-pour after we put the columns in at no charge, but Meredith said not to worry about it. He said he's gonna have the architect redo the design and make that part a sort of outdoor patio area or something. Ain't no skin off my nose. We get paid the same no matter what."

I began to get a glimmer of an idea. Meredith didn't strike me as the type to cave easily, not even to pressure from a labor union. Maybe he gave in because he'd achieved what he was after, and what I needed was under that slab of concrete. I needed more than a hunch, though, to prove it.

"How much trouble would it be to remove that concrete?" I asked.

"Well, if we'd done it right away, not too much," he said. "But, it's set pretty good now. Taking it out, rebar and all, would take my whole crew of ten a couple of days maybe. Why? You thinking Meredith's changed his mind and wants it out?"

No way in hell would Meredith want that done. Not if my hunch was right.

"No, I was just curious. Say, thanks for your help."

I turned to walk away, and saw a silver Audi A6 pull up in front of my Volkswagen. A red-faced, angry looking Jackson Meredith was behind the wheel. He got out, slamming the door behind him, and stalked over to us.

"What the fuck you doing here, Pennyback?" he asked in a stormy voice. He pointed over his shoulder with his thumb. "And, why is that little weasel Cooper with you?"

With a puzzled expression on his face, Wozniak looked from me to Meredith.

"I'm just going where the leads take me," I said. Let him ponder the meaning of that.

"How's coming out here helping you find my wife? And, what does Cooper have to do with it?"

"Hey, you said you was hired to check on company operations," Wozniak said.

Meredith whirled on him. "Wha-, whaddya mean he was checking on operations, what operations?"

"Uh, he just asked about the . . . work stoppage is all."

Eyes narrowed to slits, Meredith turned back to glare at me.

"Why would you be interested in that?" His voice was low and full of menace. "That's got nothing to do with Caroline."

"Look, Meredith," I said. "I think you and I should go somewhere we can talk in private."

"Nothing wrong with right here," he said. He pointed at Wozniak. "You're the guy in charge, right . . . Wiz something—"

"Wozniak, Mike Wozniak, and yeah I'm—"

"Yeah, yeah, Wozniak, got it. Now get your guys back to work."

Meredith turned away, dismissing the construction foreman with the same air of superiority some people use on panhandlers. This guy had a lot to learn about how to treat people, and it was time for his first lesson.

"Okay, I guess this is private enough," I said. "Your question about why I came here; well, that's because I think your wife's . . . absence, is related to your partner's disappearance."

He took a step back, and his face paled. There was a flicker of fear in his eyes, but he recovered quickly.

"What the flaming fuck are you talking about? How can Noah stealing the company blind and skipping be related to my wife's asshole of a father helping her hide from me?"

He'd recovered, but he still had a problem of controlling his outbursts. So, Caroline's father was helping her 'hide from him.' Now, why would that be, I wondered? I decided to poke the hornets' nest a bit more and see what flew out.

"I haven't completely worked out the timeline yet," I said. "But, here's what I think happened. I think you stole money from your own company to cover your gambling debt to Vinnie D'Angelo, and when your partner discovered it and confronted you about it, you killed him." The muscles under both eyes were pulsing like crazy, and I saw micro-tremors in his lips. "Then, I think somehow your wife found out about it, and you threatened to kill her. Must have happened while you were in Hong Kong, since you're certain she's still alive—which, by the way, I agree with—and her father was able to help her hide."

"You're fucking crazy. You don't have one shred of evidence to back up a wild ass story like that."

:"Oh, I'll admit I don't have all the evidence, but that's just a matter of time." I looked at the construction site. As I did, out of the corner of my eye I saw his Adam's apple bobbing up and down. "I've just got one more piece of the puzzle to put in place, and then I'll have what I need, and you, my friend, will be heading to jail."

"You g-got some nerve, you son of a bitch." Spittle flew from his mouth. "I'm paying you, and you're investigating me? You're fired! As of this moment, you're fired. And, if I see you anywhere near any WheMer property or project I'll have your ass arrested for trespass. In fact, I might just sue your ass. Now, you get out of here before I call the cops."

That was an empty threat. I seriously doubted that he wanted the police poking around this particular project. What he wanted, and he was using the threat of calling the police to get it, was for *me* not to be poking around this particular project, and I knew why. More importantly, I now knew where the body was buried. Well, at least one of the bodies.

I still had a few things to do to get Meredith properly dealt with. For that, I needed to talk to Wentworth and her partner. Then, I'd have to find Caroline Meredith.

Charles Ray

# NINETEEN

"You have got to be kidding," Daisy Wentworth said. Her partner, William Smith, just sat straddling the chair next to my bookcase with a smirk on his face. "You really expect FBI agents to go along with a crazy plan like that?"

"Well . . . yeah . . . I kind of hoped you'd think it was a good idea," I said.

I'd thought it was a pretty good idea when I came up with it the day before as I drove back from Mount Airy. It was really a pretty simple plan, and it only required a little acting on their parts, that, and a little lying.

What I wanted Wentworth and Smith to do was visit Meredith and drop the news that the FBI now thought his partner had been murdered, perhaps by some criminal element—best not to be too specific there, I thought—and that they had a clue as to where the body might be buried. This was the part that required a little acting. They would need to slowly work up to the announcement that whoever had killed Noah Whelan had buried his body on one of the company's active construction projects because that's the last place the police would think to look. I told them they should watch his body language and facial expressions at this point, because he was likely to give himself away with micro-expressions of guilt. But, the kicker would be when they asked his permission to excavate a couple of the projects. I'd gotten a list of areas where construction was underway, one in Alexandria, Virginia, and another in Gaithersburg, Maryland. One of these would be mentioned, followed by the Mount Airy project, and they would just add that they might need to break up some concrete just to be sure, and to enable the cadaver sniffing dogs a better shot at locating any remains. My guess is that he would come up with some reason to say no, and then they could put more pressure on him, finally hinting that they viewed him as a person of interest. His lack of impulse control, I reckoned, would cause him to blurt out something, or blow up at them—maybe even say something incriminating.

Okay, it was a long shot, but it was better than anything they'd come up with after weeks of investigating the case. I thought Wentworth, who had acted outside the box by bringing me into the investigation, would be keen on another innovative approach, but she pushed back on every point. It might be viewed as entrapment. Meredith would know they were bluffing, and call his lawyer, and since they didn't have enough for a search warrant, they'd be stopped cold in their tracks. I couldn't be sure he'd buried Whelan in Mount Airy. It went on and on. As fast as I raised a point, she shot it down. I was becoming dispirited, and on the verge of considering giving up—considering only, because I was convinced I was right, and I can be stubborn when I think I'm right.

After an hour or argument that went nowhere, Wentworth was getting frustrated, and looked like she was about to terminate our meeting and leave, and I got a reprieve from a most unexpected corner.

"Actually, I think he might be on to something," Smith said.

I'm not sure which of us was more astonished, me or Wentworth. It was the first time Smith had shown any inclination to agree with me, or even like me for that matter.

"You can't be serious," Wentworth said.

"No, hear me out," he said. "I think Al has a point." Another first—up till now, he either called me 'Pennyback,' or just refused to use my name. "I've known lots of guys like Meredith, and bullies like him are easy to manipulate if you know how."

"B-but, this guy's killed . . . okay, I'll admit that I believe he killed his partner, but, do you think a man who'd kill his partner and bury him in a construction site—that's pretty sophisticated—will easily fall for us trying to bait him into losing his temper?"

"I don't thing putting the partner in the site was so much sophistication as opportunity," I said. "After all, he's in construction, and he knows how hard it would be to get permission to pull down a new building."

"I agree with Al," Smith said. "Hell, killing his partner was probably an impulsive act when he was confronted about the money."

Poor Winthrop sat there between us, her head swiveling from left to right as she looked from Smith to me and back again. She looked befuddled, bothered, and beleaguered, and finally, beaten down.

I looked across her at Smith, and, for the first time, recognized in him a kindred spirit. Here was someone who, like me, was predisposed to action, who, when faced with a problem, was willing to try the thing that had never been tried before. It was the old army adage the drill sergeants had pounded into us trainees incessantly from day one of basic training and beyond, 'do something, even if it's wrong.' A soldier or unit moving and doing something is a harder target to hit, and if what you're doing turns out wrong, you just do something else. When you're doing nothing, going nowhere, it's difficult to change course.

Daisy Winthrop was like a lot of people I know. She liked certainty. Without it, she was more comfortable just doing nothing. She must have been pretty sure of herself when she roped me into their investigation. But, she was outmatched now. With her partner on one side and me on the other, the two of us united against her do-nothing stance, she was caught between two irresistible objects. We were as implacable and unstoppable as two avalanches, and she was in our paths.

Daisy Winthrop was also extremely savvy. She knew when she was beaten.

"Okay, I think you're both bonkers," she said. "But, I'm willing to give it a shot. There are, however, a few ground rules I must insist on."

She then proceeded to give us her conditions; she would conduct the interview with Meredith—she agreed that if it looked like he was on the verge of blurting something out, and egging him might facilitate it, I could take a shot, our focus would be on getting him to say something that would give her justification to ask the U.S. Attorney to seek a warrant to search the project at Mount Airy. She then wanted to know what our fall back plan was if provoking Meredith didn't work.

"Uh, it'll work," I said. Another way of saying, I hadn't really thought of a Plan B. "Look, I've already provoked him by visiting the site. He was clearly nervous about my being there. If I show up at his office with two FBI agents in tow, I think the guy will freak."

Smith nodded in agreement. Wentworth finally caved, but her expression wasn't happy. As for me, my fingers were crossed, and I said a silent prayer to whatever gods protect fools and adventurers.

# TWENTY

Wentworth almost started another argument when I suggested we go right away to Meredith's office, but Smith sided with me again. She wanted to check in with the Special Agent in Charge, the SAIC, but Smith and I reminded her that the bureau was still leery about confronting Meredith without more evidence, and this foray of ours was designed to get that evidence. If the SAIC shot this idea down, we'd be left dead in the water.

Finally, she relented, but it was 11:00 am by the time we reached the WheMer offices.

The receptionist, the same arrogant woman from my first visit, started the spiel about 'needing an appointment,' but Wentworth and Smith flashed their gold FBI shields and snarled at her.

"This is FBI business," Wentworth said. "If you interfere, or call your boss to let him know we're on our way to his office, I will arrest you, and you *will* be prosecuted."

Even I knew that last was bullshit, but Wentworth said it with just the right amount of menace and gravity. The receptionist paled and looked like she wanted to crawl away to some corner and hide. As we walked away from the reception desk, I noted a slight smile on Wentworth's face.

"Pretty good acting," I whispered.

"If I'm doing this, I'm doing it all the way," she shot back.

"Well, let's do this," said Smith.

I was really beginning to like these two.

Meredith was sitting behind his oversized desk reading the *Washington Post* when we barged in. He frowned and slapped the paper down on the desk.

"What's the meaning of this? How'd you three get past reception?" He saw me. "What are you doing here? I fired you," he said, irrigating the newspaper on his desk with a fresh spray of spittle.

Wentworth approached his desk dead on, her badge held up so he could see it. Smith moved to the right and I moved left, effectively blocking Meredith behind his desk. That maneuver had been Wentworth's brainchild. She might not have been keen on the idea, but once it was decided to do it, she was executing with vigor.

"You remember me, don't you, Mr. Meredith? I'm Special Agent Daisy Wentworth. My partner and I spoke to you before about the theft of money from your company," she said.

"Oh, yeah, I remember you now. Any word on that partner of mine?" he asked. He tried to look innocent, but the beads of sweat on his face, despite the rather cool temperature of his office, told a different story.

"Not really," she replied. "We have, though, come into possession of some new information that sheds a . . . new light on the case."

"Oh, what would that be?" He shot me a suspicious look. "Uh, is it a good idea for him to be here? I mean, until very recently he was working for me."

"I'm aware of that," Wentworth said. "I understand you discharged Mr. Pennyback. So, you see, he no longer works for you. He is now helping us in our investigation."

Now, he was unable to conceal the worry that creased his features.

"What can a private dick do to help the FBI?" He leaned forward, planting his hands on his desk. His gaze never left me.

Wentworth walked up to the desk, almost touching it.

"Do you mean if we sit down, Mr. Meredith? I have a few questions I need to ask."

She moved the chair until it was centered, and sat, primly crossing her legs and staring levelly at him.

Meredith's gaze moved from me to her, and kept moving until it came to Smith who was standing at the side of the desk with his arms folded across his massive chest and looking at Meredith as if he was studying a particularly icky specimen in biology lab. I thought Smith's pose and expression were sufficiently intimidating, so I copied him. Finally, Meredith flopped back in his chair. The leather cushioned seat made a whooshing sound.

"Okay," he said. "But, I don't know what more I can tell you that I haven't already."

"Well now, Mr. Meredith, when we spoke to you before, we were operating on the assumption that your partner, Noah Whelan, had stolen the five million dollars you say is missing, and had fled to Florida where, unfortunately, we lost the trail."

"Yeah, that's what happened." His brow was creased, and the beads of sweat had turned into small streams that flowed down his cheeks.

"No, Mr. Meredith, that's *not* what happened."

He looked like he was choking on his tongue as he fought not to react to that little bombshell. I had to give Wentworth credit. She was playing this for all it was worth, and from the way the ends of her mouth kept twitching, she seemed to be enjoying the heck out of it.

"You see, what we think is that Mr. Whelan never left Washington. Instead, we think someone who looked enough like him to get past TSA at the airport, was paid to fly to Miami just to mislead us."

"What?" Meredith feigned surprise. "You mean he paid someone to use his name and driver's license to make everyone think he was leaving town, but didn't?"

"No, that's not what I mean. I . . . we think someone else paid the double, and that the same someone killed Mr. Whelan."

"That doesn't make any sense," Meredith said. "Who would want to kill Noah?"

"That's what we're trying to determine. As soon as we find the body and examine it, we should get a clue as to who did it."

"Y-you think you know where the body is?" If looks could kill, I would have keeled over from the glance he threw my way. He was sweating so much now his jacket had dark half-moons at his armpits.

Wentworth had the hook in deep. Now it was time to set it and start reeling him in.

"Yes," she said. "We have a good idea. We think someone buried him at one of your company's construction sites, thinking no one would ever think to look there."

His eyes went wide and his mouth drooped open.

"And, we want to do some digging to

confirm that," Smith put in.

Meredith's face went pale.

"W-which sites are you talking about?"

"Well, there's the office building in Alexandria," Wentworth said. "We'd like your okay to get a team in there."

Meredith smiled. "No problem, when would you like to do it?"

"As soon as possible," she said. "There's one other site we'd like to check." Meredith's worried look came back. "The shopping mall project in . . . where was it, Agent Smith?"

"Mount Airy," Smith said.

"Uh, well, that might be a problem," Meredith said. "We've had some labor issues up there, and we're already behind schedule."

"We know about that," Smith said. "But, the office project in Virginia is even further along. If we start digging in there, it's gonna be set back a hell a lot further than a shopping center, don't you think?"

"So far, all you have up in Mount Airy is a partial concrete pad and a few concrete pillars," I chimed in. "Shouldn't take but a day or two to get cadaver dogs in there. Won't take nearly as long as the office building." I looked down at Wentworth. "In fact, in the interest of saving time, I think you should check there first."

Meredith was really fighting now to maintain his composure, but panic was written all over his face.

"N-no . . . look, you have to understand

how these things work. The union up there is out of Baltimore, and . . . well, you just don't mess with those guys."

"I think the FBI is capable of dealing with a local labor union," Wentworth said.

"Well, there's the t-technical issues as w-well," he said.

"What technical issues?" she asked.

"I can show you on the plans," he said. "If you'll just wait here, I'll get them."

She nodded.

He stood and squeezed between Smith and the desk, heading for the door. Wentworth remained seated, but Smith and I shared a look. He was thinking the same thing I was; Meredith, the dumb bastard, was actually thinking about running.

I've never understood crooks. They get cornered, and if they get the chance, they run. Contrary to what you see on TV or in the movies, they seldom get far. And, Meredith, for all his size, wasn't in anything like the shape of the actors playing bad guys in most of the movies I'd seen. That, and the fact that his building was in the middle of a large parking lot, just off U.S. 1, with a shopping center about half a mile north, a small strip mall across the street, and vacant lots to the south. In other words, he didn't have anywhere to run. He could make a run for his Audi, but the FBI's Chevy Suburban had a souped-up engine that would run him down before he'd gone a block. In his case, running was doubly stupid, because it was as good as an admission of guilt.

I beat Smith to the door, and as I exited, I saw Meredith, legs pumping, heading down the hallway toward the reception area.

"Damnit, I hate it when they run," Smith said as he came out of the office behind me.

"He won't get far," I said.

"Oh, I know that, but despite the cold weather, I sweat when I run, and it wrinkles the hell out of my clothes."

I laughed. I hadn't thought of Smith as fashion conscious. "Don't sweat it—pun intended—I'll catch him."

"You have my permission to bruise him a little," he said.

I took off after Meredith. By the time I got to the reception area, he was out the door and heading for his car, which was parked at the near corner of the building. I put on the speed, exited the building, and caught up with him just as he reached for the driver-side door.

He was in such a state, his hand slipped off the door handle, and he fell against the body of the car, giving me enough time to grab his shoulder.

"Hold up, friend," I said. "You're not going anywhere."

He spun around, pushing at my chest.

"Get your fucking hands off me you son of a bitch." He looked around. Smith hadn't emerged from the building. He smiled wickedly. "You're not a cop, so get the fuck away from me."

"Wrong, bucko. I'm making a citizen's arrest. So just stand down until the feds get here with handcuffs."

He shoved harder, and looked a bit surprised that I wasn't pushed back.

"I told you to get the fuck away from me," he shouted.

"Look, this can go easy, or it can go hard; it's up to you. Frankly, I don't care one way or the other."

"You want it hard, I'll give you hard," he said, and began reaching into his jacket with his right hand.

I assumed he was reaching for a weapon. That was a major mistake on his part. We were too close together, close enough that I had an advantage. I slipped my left hand down and grasped his right wrist, my fingers on the back of his hand and my thumb pressed into his wrist at the base of his thumb. I pressed as hard as I could. It got the desired result. His hand stopped moving and he squealed, making a sound like fingernails scratching across a chalk board. While his attention was on the pain I knew was shooting up his arm, I brought my right hand up to cheek level and slammed my fist against the end of his nose. The blow hit his nose and upper lip, squashing the former and splitting the latter. Bright red blood spurted from his nose and cut lip, and his squeal morphed into a gurgling sound. His eyes clenched shut and his left hand reached up to his mangled face as his body sagged against the Audi and slid slowly to the asphalt.

Just as I was reaching into his coat to remove his weapon, Smith came trotting up. I pulled out a snub-nose .38 pearl-handled revolver and held it up for Smith.

"Shit, the son of a bitch was packing heat," he said as he took it. He smiled down at the moaning Meredith. "You bruised him good. I hope that felt good."

I smiled and rubbed the knuckles of my right hand.

"It did, it really did."

# TWENTY-ONE

Meredith's attempt to flee when the subject of the Mount Airy project was mentioned was enough for Wentworth and Smith to get a warrant to dig under the concrete pad at the construction site. The search began the next day, Wednesday, at 8:30 am. The concrete was removed by 10:50, and a cadaver dog focused on a spot within ten minutes. At 11:42, the remains of Noah Whelan, a single gunshot wound in the center of his forehead, were exhumed.

Once the body was found, and it was clear that there hadn't been any interstate travel, the FBI surrendered the case to the local authorities, with the Maryland State Police taking the lead since the body had been found in that state, but with the Washington

Metropolitan Police Department playing an important role because it was suspected that the crime took place in the District.

The remains were taken to the medical examiner's office in the District at 1:00 pm, and an autopsy was begun immediately. The first order of business was finding and removing the slug, which was still in fairly good shape despite having pierced the frontal bone of the skull. While a full autopsy would be conducted, that lump of lead, lodged in the victim's brain, was a pretty clear cause of death.

The slug was identified by the DC forensics lab as a .36 caliber hollow point, and when it was compared to one test fired from the weapon taken from Meredith, it was clear that both slugs had been fired from the same barrel. This evidence was obtained at 4:00 pm.

At 4:52 pm, Meredith, dressed in the orange jump suit of a prisoner of the District of Columbia Corrections Authority, was led into Interview Room 1 at the MPD Fifth District on Bladensburg Road in Northeast DC. A team of homicide detectives, led by my buddy, Detective 1 Buster Mayweather, who had been recently promoted to lieutenant, came from downtown to conduct the initial interview, which would be done by Buster and a burly detective sergeant named O'Brien. Wentworth, Smith, and I were allowed to observe through the one-way glass set in the wall of a large, sparsely furnished adjacent room.

Meredith was accompanied by a seedy looking character, with slicked down blond hair combed forward in a vain attempt to hide his rapidly receding hairline, wearing a gray pinstriped suit that probably cost more than my monthly retirement check from the army. Gordon Jenkins was Meredith's attorney of record. I didn't know him personally, but I'd heard of him. He had a reputation for representing some really unsavory characters.

Everyone arranged themselves at a plain metal institutional table, done in shades of gray, with a goose-neck microphone attached to the middle that could be adjusted to record from any position at the table. Buster pulled the mike toward him, while Jenkins fussed with some papers in the expensive leather attaché case he carried. Meredith sat wooden, staring across the table at Buster.

Finally, Buster tapped the microphone. A loud thumping sound came from the speakers on the walls near us.

"November 27, 2002, at 5:12 pm. This is Detective Lieutenant Buster Mayweather and Detective Sergeant Lawrence O'Brien, and we're at Metropolitan Police Department Fifth District, interviewing Mr. Jackson Meredith. Mr. Meredith is accompanied by his attorney, Mr. Gordon Jenkins," Buster said.

"Uh, detective, I really need more time

with my client before we do this," Jenkins said.

"You've had over an hour with your client, Mr. Jenkins. This is just a preliminary interview. You can have more time with him after we take him downtown and book him. Now, Mr. Meredith, were you read your Miranda rights when you were arrested?"

Meredith glared at Buster. "Yeah," he said.

"Did you understand those rights?"

"Yeah, what's to understand?" Some of Meredith's bluster had come back, although, with the split and puffed upper lip, and the butterfly bandage on his nose—turned out I broke it when I smacked him—he didn't look too imposing.

"Let it be shown that Mr. Meredith has been advised of his rights, and he understands them," Buster said. "Now, Mr. Meredith, do you own a .38 caliber pistol?"

Before Meredith could answer, Jenkins laid a hand on his arm and leaned in to whisper something to him. Meredith frowned and brushed the hand away.

"Hell, they already know that," he said. He turned to Buster. "Yeah, I have a .38. I have to travel to a lot of construction sites around the area, some of them in some pretty rough neighborhoods, so I bought it for protection."

"Could you explain why you've never applied for a license, or why we can't find a namecheck record on you in the ATF database for that weapon?"

Meredith's cheeks reddened.

"I guess I must've forgot to register it," he said. "As for a purchase record, I bought it at a gun show in Charlottesville, Virginia, so there was no requirement for a namecheck."

I saw the muscles in Buster's shoulders stiffen. That little loophole in the law was the reason for a good number of the guns on the District's streets. At gun shows, people could sell all manner of firearms without the federal namecheck or mandatory waiting requirement, and there was often no records made of the sales, making it damn near impossible to trace the history of a weapon unless it had been used in a previous crime.

"And, this .38 is the one taken from you by FBI Agent William Smith earlier today at your office on Rhode Island Avenue?"

"Actually, it was that shit heel, Pennyback, that took it from me," he said.

"You're referring to Mr. Albert Pennyback, the private detective who was helping the FBI?"

Meredith made a snarling noise and tried to sneer, but the split in his upper lip was too painful, so he ended up making a spitting sound and wincing. "Yeah, that's him," he said finally. He turned to his lawyer. "Can we sue that fucker for assault? He broke my nose."

"If I understand what happened," Buster said before Jenkins could answer. "You were in the process of fleeing the FBI and Mr.

Pennyback was asked by the agents to assist in your capture. When he caught up to you, you started to draw your weapon, and he took defensive steps to prevent that."

"I wasn't *fleeing,* I—"

Buster held up a meaty hand to stop him. "Mr. Meredith, you were running full speed from your building, and just about to get into your vehicle when Mr. Pennyback caught up to you. How is that not fleeing to avoid arrest?"

"Don't answer that, Jackson," his lawyer admonished.

Meredith clamped his mouth shut.

"Okay, let's address another subject," Buster said. "You told the police and the FBI that your partner, the late Noah Whelan, stole five million dollars from the company accounts and fled, is that correct?"

Meredith and Jenkins conducted a whispered conference. When they concluded, Meredith smiled at Buster. "Actually, what I told the authorities was that five million dollars was missing, and that I didn't know my partner's whereabouts. They came to the conclusion that he stole the money and ran away."

I looked at Wentworth.

"Yeah, he's actually right there," she said. "Of course, the way he told us, it was clear what his meaning was."

I suppose that meant something to them, but I wasn't worried that he'd be able to wriggle his way out of the corner Buster was painting him into.

"That's as it may be," Buster said, his voice clear over the speaker. "But, you have admitted that the .38 taken from you is, in fact, yours, right?"

"Yeah, I guess I did."

Meredith's lawyer was beginning to look nervous. Unlike his client, he had a few operating brain cells, and it looked like he saw which way the train was heading. He jerked at the sleeve of Meredith's orange jump suit, only to have his hand knocked away.

"Well, Mr. Meredith," Buster continued. "You'll be interested to know that Noah Whelan didn't flee town. In fact, we found him this morning."

Meredith looked confused. "Huh?" he said.

"Yes, we found him. Well, more accurately, we found his body, and would you like to guess where we found it?"

"Shut up, Jackson." Jenkins had his hand on his client's shoulder, grasping so hard his knuckles were white. "You don't have to answer that question," he said in a stage whisper that came clearly over the speaker.

"What's the harm," the still clueless Meredith said. "I mean, I don't know the answer to his question, so my answer would be no, I wouldn't like to guess."

Jenkins rolled his eyes and sat back in his chair. I was willing to bet that at that moment he was regretting ever having taken on Meredith as a client.

"Oh, you don't have to guess," Buster said. "I'll tell you. We found Noah Whelan's body under a slab of concrete at your construction site in Mount Airy . . . a slab of concrete that you had a bunch of temporary laborers pour after you caused the regular construction crew to go on strike."

Meredith was slow, really slow, but even his sluggish brain was capable of eventually receiving and interpreting a clear signal. He could now see which the train was heading, and he was standing frozen right in the middle of the tracks.

"Wha-," he said. He looked lost and confused. He turned to his lawyer.

Jenkins held his hands up, palms out, waving him off. "Don't look at me," he said. "I told you to keep your mouth shut, but no-o-o, you just have to talk. Well, you talked yourself into this, so talk yourself out."

Talk like that, if it ever got the Bar Association, wouldn't go down well for Mr. Jenkins, but he was obviously so exasperated with his client he no longer cared. Buster had his back to me, but I didn't need to see his face to know he was smiling. He leaned forward, prepared for the *coup de grace*.

"That's not all, Mr. Meredith," he said. "The coroner took a bullet out of Mr. Whelan's brain. You want to guess what weapon that bullet is a perfect match for? No, that's okay, you don't have to guess. Your .38 is the gun used to kill Noah Whelan. Would you care to make a comment on that?"

Looking like a man who's just farted and discovered that the bubbling sound that accompanied his flatulence wasn't air, Meredith slumped down in his chair. He turned to his lawyer.

"I'm not saying another word," he said. "You got any more questions, you talk to my lawyer."

Sad-eyed, Gordon Jenkins looked at his client. "You should have led with that line, Jackson."

Buster and O'Brien stood.

"You know, the FBI only detained you," Buster said. "And, then they turned you over to us for disposition. Now, I'm disposing." He looked over his shoulder at the one-way mirror and smiled wolfishly. "Jackson Meredith, I'm placing you under the arrest for the murder of Noah Whelan, and the theft of five million dollars from WheMer. You have the right to remain silent, if—"

"Fuck all that," Meredith said. "Take me to my cell."

Charles Ray

# TWENTY-TWO

Thanksgiving dinner the next day at Buster's house in the District was festive. Sandra and I arrived at 11:30 because Sandra wanted to help Alma with dinner preparations. It was a chance for Buster and me to sit on his sun porch and have a before dinner aperitif or two. Unfortunately, the twins, little Albert and Sandra, were past the toddler stage, and loved nothing more than jumping on Uncle Al's lap and pulling his ears. It took a few minutes for Buster to convince them to go to the playroom just off the living room and play with their old toys—because, Christmas was just around the corner, and they'd be getting new stuff—so daddy and Uncle Al could talk business. I don't ever remember my son Ethan falling for such a hokey story, but it worked on the twins.

When they were out of sight, Buster got two Budweisers from the small fridge he kept in the sunroom, and handed one to me.

"Here's to the successful conclusion of a case, bro," he said.

"Yeah, it is nice to see scum like Jackson Meredith behind bars," I said.

"And, just think, he paid you for most of it."

"I think he's sitting in his cell right now, ruing the day he ever walked into my office."

"Did you ever find out who referred him to you?"

"No, and he refused to tell me."

"That dude gives shit to everyone," he said. "Say, did you ever get a lead on finding his dead wife?" He laughed so hard after saying that, he sprayed beer all over the floor.

He'd thought from the beginning that it was a crazy, time-waster of a case. I debated sharing my theory with him, but something made me hesitate.

You see, just as I'd concluded that Noah Whelan was dead, despite having not one shred of evidence to support that belief, I'd come to the conclusion that Caroline Meredith hadn't died in that auto crash. There was nothing to support that thesis, just my gut feeling. But, I trusted my gut feelings. They'd saved my ass more than once.

It was my first of two tours in Vietnam, in the turbulent time right after the disastrous 1968 Tet Offensive. I'd been assigned to a long-range recon outfit supporting II Corps, working out of a Quonset hut near the Corps headquarters in Pleiku, and running recon missions throughout the Central Highlands. Our six-man and twelve-man teams were led by company grade officers, lieutenants or junior captains, or senior noncoms. As one of the senior-most junior captains in the outfit, I had my choice of teams. I took command of RF-Birddog—eleven experienced recon soldiers who had been together for eight months when I took command.

After a week in command, with four successful patrols under my belt, I was feeling comfortable in the new job. Then, one day, the unit commander, an infantry lieutenant colonel two years away from retirement, and no chance in hell of making bird colonel, ordered my unit to go into Chu Pau Pass, a mountainous area halfway between Pleiku and Kontum, to check on reports that a main force NVA unit had come over into the area from the Cambodian-Laotian-Vietnamese border area. If true, it meant the road between the two provincial towns could be interdicted.

My first reaction after the colonel had finished talking was that the thing to do was send a couple of battalions in to do a recon in force. The terrain between Pleiku and

Kontum was hilly and covered by thick vegetation, elephant grass and low-growing trees, making it difficult to see anything from the air, and on the ground, the vegetation was so lush and grew so close to the road, the VC and NVA could be lying in ambush a few meters off the road and a US or ARVN convoy wouldn't see them until the first AK-47 or RPG round popped.

It was also a hellacious place to patrol. If you used the trails, you left yourself open to ambush. If you moved off the trails, you were lucky to make a kilometer an hour it was so thick. It was also difficult to move through the brush without making noise. What I didn't want to do was prove the colonel's theory by losing half my men.

At the same time, I couldn't just refuse the mission. So, with the help of my senior NCO, Dave Tutko, a master sergeant who'd seen service in Korea, I came up with a plan. The team moved out from Pleiku at first light, kept to the main road for the first two kilometers, and then moved west into the bush. Our plan was to move a kilometer or so, stop and get our bearings, then move again. The colonel wanted us to make it a two-day mission, but that would have meant risking making noise. I figured if we pinpointed the NVA location, he'd forgive me for taking longer than he wanted. If he didn't, it didn't matter—my troops would still be alive.

Things went well for the first two days of the mission, but on the third day, as we moved out of our night bivouac position, I began to feel strange. Not sick strange, more like that itchy feeling you get when something's about to go wrong. When I mentioned it to Tutko, he advised me to trust my gut.

I halted the team and had everyone take up positions on either side of the clearing we'd been traveling through. It was a game trail that meandered through the forest, but it went in the general direction we wanted, and it beat beating the bush by a mile.

After making sure everyone was properly concealed, locked and loaded, I hunkered down behind a hummock of earth with Tutko, and the two of us scanned the jungle ahead. The only sound was the chattering of monkeys in the trees above us.

Then, the monkeys stopped chattering. The silence was palpable, weighing on me like a heavy wool blanket. They'd gotten use to our presence, but something had disturbed them.

Time has a way of slowing down at some critical moments in life. This was one of them. It felt like we'd crouched there forever behind that hummock, the humid heat of the forest cloaking us in sweat, and attracting the little gnats and larger dragon flies that we didn't dare swat at for fear of making a sound. I could feel my heart beating in my chest.

When the first little guy wearing the dusty green uniform and campaign helmet of an NVA regular stepped into the far side of the clearing, I felt a strange sense of relief. The waiting was finally over.

I'd given my men an order to wait for me to fire first, so Tutko and I waited. A second soldier emerged from the thicket, and another, and another, until a file of five were walking directly toward us. They walked by without noticing us. I waited until the fifth man had passed our position, before bringing my M-16 up to my shoulder and loosing a three-round burst into him. The impact of the three 5.56 rounds punching into his lower back sent him stumbling into the man in front of him. By the time the remaining four NVA could react, though, my entire team had cut loose, hitting them from both sides. The shooting was over in less than two minutes. The five NVA were bloody, tattered corpses on the forest floor, having gotten off only two or three wild rounds before we cut them down.

We searched the bodies, finding documents that would have to be translated by the G-2 types back at Pleiku, but from the symbols and numbers I assumed it identified the unit moving into our area.

The colonel did forgive me for taking longer than *he* wanted, especially since the II Corps commander was happy that we'd located the enemy unit, and the colonel got a letter of commendation for it. My unit got nothing, not even a two day R&R, but at least they were alive. Thanks to my gut for giving me early warning—had we kept moving, we would have likely been on the receiving end of an ambush—and thanks to Dave Tutko for convincing me to trust my gut.

"No, just as you predicted, that case turned into a dead end," I said.

Recognizing his own lame pun being turned back on him, Buster laughed.

"Yeah, and now that your client's in jail, you're not getting paid to chase ghosts," he said.

"Yeah, there is that."

I hated withholding things from him. I hadn't quit the case. But, I also hadn't decided what I was going to do when I found Caroline Meredith. And, I had no doubt that I would find her. No one can hide forever.

# TWENTY-THREE

I mulled over the problem for several days, dropping it only for the weekend to spend some quality time with Sandra. Back in my office on Monday, December 2, I plopped down in my chair, booted up my laptop, took out a notepad and pen, and determined to seriously tackle the dilemma of the missing, presumed dead (but, not by me) Caroline Meredith.

After checking my emails, and deleting them all, I turned my attention to the notebook. Its empty page seemed to stare up at me with an accusatory expression. I wrote, 'WHERE IS CAROLINE MEREDITH?,' across the top of the page just so it wouldn't be blank, but it still seemed to be mocking me.

Have you ever stared at an inanimate

object, trying to mentally force it to do your bidding? Well, the old saying, 'a watched pot never boils,' is pretty accurate—at least, not until the water reaches the boiling point. That damned page was the same. No matter how hard I stared at it, or how I strained for answers to my question to appear, that single line of my crabby writing was all there was.

I finally decided there was only one thing to do; I'd go out to Germantown and confront Matt Donahue. I would make him tell me where he'd stashed his daughter, and put this thing to rest once and for all.

"Where are you going in such a huff?" Heather asked as I headed for the door.

"I'm going to Germantown," I said.

It took her a few seconds to make the connection.

"Go easy on the old man, Al," she said. "You could be wrong, you know, and pushing him on it would only add to his grief."

Believe me, I'd thought about that. But, I was convinced that I was right.

"Don't worry, I'll go easy on him. Maybe now that Meredith's in jail, he'll be willing to talk."

That would be my first approach. If that didn't work . . . well, it just had to work.

An hour later I pulled into Matt Donahue's driveway. As I got out of the car, a gust of wind pulled at my jacket. It was truly December, with the temperature dropping into the high 30s by mid-morning, and continuing to dip until dark. I pulled my jacket tighter and rang his doorbell.

When Matt Donahue opened the door and saw me his face fell. I stepped up and put a foot on the sill just in case he was thinking of closing it in my face.

"What are you doing here? I already said all I have to say to you," he said.

"I'm sorry to bother you again, Mr. Donahue, but I have a few more questions about your daughter's . . . accident."

He clenched his lips and swallowed hard, looking at a space a foot to the right of my head.

"There's nothing more I can tell you. Why don't you go away and let me mourn in peace."

I squeezed past him. He didn't move to stop me. He just stood there looking at me with a forlorn look on his craggy face.

"Well, you see, Matt . . . you mind if I call you Matt?" He didn't respond, so I took that as an okay. "You see, Matt, that's just the problem. For a man who recently lost his daughter in a terrible accident, you really don't look like you're in mourning."

He blinked rapidly and looked away from me again.

"What the hell do you mean by that?" He spoke to me without looking *at* me.

I didn't feel good about what I was doing to him. But, if I was right, he'd done something wrong—done it for the right reasons, but wrong nonetheless.

"You mind if we sit down?" I asked.

He nodded toward the sofa, and then sat in the large chair facing it.

"Okay," he said. "We're sitting, now you mind telling me what the hell you're doing here?"

I could have just hit him between the eyes with it, but he *was* a combat veteran, and I still respected that. Besides that, I figured he'd done whatever it was he'd done to protect his daughter. In his shoes, I might have done the same.

"You might not have heard, but the cops arrested your son-in-law last week. He's being charged with the murder of his partner."

That got his attention. He looked at me with wide eyes.

"I always knew that bastard was no good, that's why . . ."

He snapped his mouth shut. He'd almost let it out. I could tell from the look in his eyes that he *wanted* to come clean, so I decided to string it out a little longer.

"Yeah. Turns out, Meredith stole money from the company, and when his partner discovered it and confronted him, he killed him and buried his body at one of his construction sites. Then, he let the cops think his partner stole the money and went on the lam."

"How'd the cops figure out it was him?"

"Like you said, Meredith was a real bad guy. He treated one of his employees unfairly, and the guy provided me with some information that led us to the body. After we confronted him with the body and forensic evidence linking him to the death, he finally broke down and confessed. He's pretty sure to get convicted, and while the District of Columbia doesn't have the death penalty, the murder to cover up his theft will get him a life sentence for sure."

"He'll probably get out on parole," he said. "He's got money, and people with money always find a way to game the system."

"I don't think so. See, he made the mistake of killing his partner in the District, and then moving the body to Maryland. That makes it interstate, and the FBI gets involved . . . got involved when they thought the partner had stolen the money and fled to Florida. I think the U.S. Justice Department's gonna be all over this case. He'll probably get life without possibility of parole."

A look of relief flickered on his face.

"So, he won't be able to hurt anybody else? That's good to hear."

"Can I tell you a story?" He looked at me, but kept silent. "Here's what I think. I think maybe someone else found out that he stole that money, and maybe even that he killed his partner, and I think that someone feared for their life, so they ran away too. That sound like anyone you know?"

It took a few seconds for my words to sink in. His face went through several changes, from wariness to weariness, and he finally sank back in the chair and let out a long sigh.

"Yeah, it does kinda sound like someone I know," he said finally. He clenched his fists. "Look, I did what I had to do. Caroline saw him come home late one night with mud all over his shoes, and blood spatters on his overcoat. When she asked him about it, he made up some dumb story about having an accident on a building site, but she didn't believe it. Then, when word got out about that guy Noah Whelan stealing company money and disappearing, she put two and two together. She figured he knew she suspected him, and she was scared, I mean real scared, that he might do the same to her, so that night after he went to sleep, she slipped out of the house and came here and told me everything."

"I can understand that, but it would have been better if she'd gone to the police."

"I told her that," he said. "But, she was just too scared. She figured with all his money, he'd be able to wheedle his way out of it, and come after her for telling. Frankly, I wouldn't have put it past him. A man who could kill a partner he's been close to for years over money, who knows what he might do."

Now, all I had to do was have him voluntarily tell me what he'd done, and my conscience would be clear. I still wasn't sure what I'd do about it, but I couldn't bring myself to attack him directly.

"So, what did she decide to do?"

"It wasn't her decided," he said. "It was all on me. She's all I got left, and I wasn't about to let anything happen to her. You got kids?"

"I had a son," I said. "He and his mother were killed in an auto accident when he was six."

"I'm sorry to hear that, but you know how it is. You'd do anything to protect your kid . . . and, I mean *anything*."

"You want to tell me about it?"

"I . . . yeah . . . I know it was wrong, but it's been eating at me ever since. I'll tell you all about it, but I think maybe Sheldon ought to be here to explain exactly how it went down."

"Your nephew, Sheldon Logan?"

"Uh-huh, but before I call him, you got to promise me one thing. You got to promise me he'll be kept out of it. It was all my doing, and I don't want nobody else to get in trouble. You promise?"

"Look, I can't promise that," I said. "But, I do promise to do all I can to minimize the damage."

I don't know what that meant, or what I could do, but it seemed to give him some ease.

"I expected you to say that. I'll say this about you, Al, you strike me as a man of honor, so I'll take your word. Let me go call, Sheldon and then we can talk."

# TWENTY-FOUR

It took an hour and a half for Sheldon Logan to get from Damascus to Germantown. Donahue and I spent that time sitting in his living room, drinking coffee and telling war stories. I'd been worried that he would be put off by my exposing his little scheme, but he seemed relieved now that it was out in the open. The sound of a car pulling into the driveway interrupted a story he was telling about the breakout from the Chosin Reservoir.

"That sounds like Sheldon's old Ford," he said. He rose and went to the door.

When he opened the door, Sheldon Logan, wearing faded jeans, a red and black plaid shirt, and a dark blue North Face jacket, walked in. He was followed by a woman his height, but with curves where his body was angular, wearing a pair of hip and leg-hugging brown pants and a tan sweater that showed her pendulous breasts to good advantage. She carried a black windbreaker over her arm. Her oval face was flushed from the cold air. Her ash blonde hair was tied back in a ponytail which gave her round blue eyes a wide-opened, surprised look, which turned into real surprise when she saw me.

"Uh, dad, you didn't say you had company," she said.

She hung back behind Logan, but her curves showed around his lanky frame.

"Come on in, you two," Donahue said. "This here's—"

"Mr. Pennyback," Logan said. "Nice seeing you again. Caroline, this is the private detective I told you about."

"It's a pleasure meeting you, Ms. Meredith," I said. "Good to see you're in good health."

She looked confused, and a bit afraid.

"What's going on?" she asked.

"You better come in and sit down, hon," Donahue said. "Mr. Pennyback knows pretty much what happened. I wanted Sheldon to tell him how we did it. He's gonna help us."

She didn't look convinced. For that matter, neither did Logan. But, they both came in and sat on the sofa. Donahue offered me his chair, but I refused, choosing to stand off to the side.

Logan looked from me to Donahue. "You want me to tell him everything, Uncle Matt?"

"Yeah, he can't help us if he doesn't have the whole picture. So, why don't you start telling him, and I'll go make a pot of coffee."

Without waiting for Logan to respond, Donahue went toward the back of the house.

"Okay, Mr. Pennyback," Logan said. "Where do I start?"

"How about at the beginning," I said.

And, that's just what he did.

He recounted, with her help, the story Caroline told her father about Meredith coming home with muddy shoes and blood on his jacket, and how she suspected foul play when she heard later that Noah Whelan was missing. She'd known from the start of their marriage that her husband had a gambling problem, and that he was often in debt because of it. She'd confronted him about the muddy shoes, and hadn't believed his story about a workplace accident.

After news broke about Whelan, she said she caught him looking strangely at her, and on the day she finally left, he'd said something about bad things happening to people who crossed him. Whether he was referring to Whelan or her she didn't know, but she decided not to take chances, so that night after he'd fallen asleep, she grabbed a few essentials and as much cash as she could find, and drove to her father's house.

When dear old dad made the decision to

help her escape her husband's clutches, or whatever else he had in mind for her, he called good old Cousin Sheldon and asked him to help.

Logan's description of how they faked her death sounded like the script of a B movie, a black comedy at that.

It took him two days to come up with a plan, one that was aided by Ronald Reagan cutting funding for mental health in the 1980s, which resulted in thousands of people who really needed to be institutionalized being turned out on the streets, swelling the ranks of the homeless geometrically. Many of the new breed of panhandlers were women, a lot were drug addicts, and most had mental or emotional problems. When the homeless died from exposure, depressingly common during cold weather, there was usually no one to claim the bodies, so they were buried as indigents by the city or state unfortunate enough to be the site of their demise. Many of them died as unknowns, and ended up either in unmarked graves in the equivalent of Potter's Field, or were cremated. It turned out that a homeless woman who regularly panhandled near the intersection of routes 27 and 108 died one night from exposure, and the body was brought to the hospital where Logan worked.

While he was examining her, he noticed that cleaned up she was a dead ringer for Caroline. That term brought laughter from everyone, including Donahue, who had come back during the story with a carafe of coffee and four cups. Since the body would only be cremated, Logan got a colleague at the hospital—whose name he refused to divulge—to help him fake the cremation paperwork. They then cleaned up the corpse and dressed her in Caroline's clothing, and that same colleague, and a cousin who owned a trucking company near Germantown, helped him put the body in Caroline's car and ran it into a utility pole. The same cousin then called the police to report the accident, while Logan and his hospital colleague made their way back to Damascus, where Caroline was staying at Logan's house.

When he finished his story, I just sat there looking at them, three anxious looking faces staring back at me.

Finally, Donahue broke the silence. "So, what do you think, Al? I know what we did was wrong, but are we in a lot of trouble, do you think?"

Hell, I'm no lawyer, nor am I a cop. I figure they'd broken several laws: desecration of a corpse or something, filing a false accident report, just for starters. Under the circumstances, I would imagine—hope—that the authorities would cut them some slack. What they needed was a good lawyer. I wondered if Quincy and his firm would take them on.

"Well, I have to say, when I first figured out that you folks had faked the accident, I was worried you might have . . . you know, killed someone to be Caroline's stand-in. Now, what you did wasn't right, but you didn't hurt anyone," I said. "I don't know how the local authorities might look at it, but if you have a good lawyer, I'm sure something could be worked out."

"Shit," Donahue said. "I don't have the money for a lawyer. I'm living on my military retirement."

"I don't suppose with Jackson in jail awaiting trial for stealing from his company, I'd be able to avail myself of that money," Caroline said. "And, I don't know how much is in our personal bank account, but I could try to scrape together as much as possible."

"I have a friend in DC who is a crackerjack lawyer," I said. "I'm sure I could talk him into representing you for a reasonable fee." I was hoping Quincy would agree.

"I guess we can't ask for more than that," Donahue said. "I guess I need to call the police and tell them what happened."

# TWENTY-FIVE

Quincy agreed to represent the three of them, and using his pull in the area's legal system got Donahue and Logan off with twelve weeks of community service. His argument that Caroline was under duress because of a valid belief that her murderous husband intended her harm, was let off with a warning. The hearing was held on the morning of December 5 in the courthouse in Rockville Town Center, and lasted less than an hour. Afterwards, the five of us gathered at Amina Thai Restaurant on Nicholson Lane in Rockville for a lunch to celebrate what was a victory for them. I never asked Quincy what he charged them, knowing he probably did it for a pittance. Holcombe, Stein and Chang does a lot of pro bono work, and Quincy does most of it. He's that kind of lawyer, one I like, and I can't say that about many in the profession.

The next day, Friday, I got more good news. Buster called to invite me to lunch at Moms. The first thing he told me after Mom had brought our coffee was that Meredith's trial date had been set for some time in late January, and that the District Attorney was going for maximum sentence—which meant life without parole—and the evidence was enough to make it stick. Meredith would be tried in the District of Columbia by a jury of his peers, which meant he was toast. With the majority of the potential jury pool in the District coming from the middle class black community, and the increasing numbers of Hispanics who had U.S. Citizenship, a rich bully like Meredith, who lost more money during a weekend in Vegas than most of the members of the jury would make in a year, he wouldn't find much sympathy. There wouldn't be many rich on the jury. Not, mind you, that I'm saying the rich buy their way out of jury duty, but in all the years I've lived in the District, I've not seen many truly rich people sitting in a jury box—behind the defense table, yeah, but not in the jury box. The prosecution was getting assistance from an unusual quarter, too. Vincent D'Angelo had been contacted by Daisy Wentworth to confirm whether or not Meredith had owed him money, and had paid his debt. Not only had the mobster confirmed that, but had gone to his lawyer in Vegas and done a signed and notarized deposition which he sent to the District Attorney by special overnight messenger.

"That mother is going down," Buster said. "I wonder what's gonna happen to his company now that he's going to jail."

As it turned out, I had the answer to that question.

"Since Caroline Meredith is still his wife and legal heir, she'll take charge of WheMer while he's in jail, which based upon what you say will be a long, long time."

"Hey, bro," he said, as he toyed with the home fried potatoes on his plate. "That's got to be one of the strangest cases you ever worked. Who else but you could go looking for a dead woman and find her alive?"

We laughed at that, and then I told him the whole story, from Caroline learning that her husband was a cold-blooded killer and thief to the faked accident with a nameless corpse that was a dead ringer for her.

"Damn, that's cold," he said after I finished. "But, I guess if little Sandra was in trouble, I'd probably do whatever I could to help her."

"That's kind of the way the judge in Rockville saw it, too, so he went easy on them. I don't know Caroline Meredith all that well, but I got a good measure of her dad, and he's a good man. I think WheMer will be in good hands from now on. She's already started it down the right path. She rehired Aaron Cooper, the engineer her husband fired."

"Sounds like good people."

I nodded my agreement and turned my attention back to the half of a breaded pork chop left on my plate.

Mom stood at her usual post by the cash register at the end of the counter, surveying her kingdom, but paying special attention to the table in the corner where Buster and I sat, like a mother hen watching over her chicks lest they stray too far. When she saw that I was dutifully cleaning my plate, she smiled. It was a broad smile that lit up her chocolate colored face. It was a smile that said she approved of what I'd done and what I was doing.

# TWENTY-SIX

Saturday, December 7, 2002 was a cold day. It was Pearl Harbor Day. A day to remember the deadly attack on our Pacific Fleet lying at anchor in Hawaii on a calm Sunday morning, unaware of the approaching Japanese bomber fleet that nearly wiped it out. It was a day with occasional wind gusts that seemed to slice through the smallest crevice in your jacket and scrape across exposed flesh like a rusty razor It was a day for staying home curled up under a blanket with a mug of hot chocolate and a good book, or with your favorite partner. It was *not* a day for pushing through the last minute Christmas shoppers in the local mall.

But, of course, that's exactly what Sandra

had us doing.

By 9:00 am, after exercising in the frigid morning air, washing, and fixing a light breakfast, we were making our way across the huge parking lot that fronted White Flint Shopping Center on Rockville Pike, already having to wend out way through hordes of other late-comers rushing toward the large, two-story entrance foyer of the mall as if worried the stores would run out of merchandise.

Christmas decorations were everywhere, and had been since the day after Thanksgiving From the huge entrance way to the sidewalks to the light poles dotted about the parking lot it was a profusion of wreaths, colorful balls, plastic trees all aglow with lights, and tinsel draped over everything. A huge Santa balloon surrounded by smaller elves and reindeer took up a large portion of the entrance, forcing people to squeeze around the sides to get to the ground floor stores or to one of the two curving stairways to stores on the upper levels. The Santa bobbed up and down and back and forth as people squeezing past jostled it, an impish smile plastered on its rubber face.

In their quest for that last-minute bargain our fellow shoppers weren't showing the Christmas spirit. They were a mean, grasping, snarling mass of inhumane humanity, in a dog-eat-dog, everyone for him or herself competition for the so-called bargains overflowing the shelves and counters, being served by harried looking salespeople who had smiles that looked as painted on as the balloon Santa's did.

We made our way through the throng to the right hand side of the first floor, dipping in and out of a jewelry store where Sandra 'oohed' and 'aahed' over baubles that she had no intention of buying, and a clothing store with odd looking garments on mannequins that looked like starved corpses, and finally gave up and muscled our way upstairs to the second level, getting our feet stepped on several times in the process.

Upstairs we stopped at a toy store. Sandra saw a complicated looking play set, a lot of odd shapes that supposedly fit together to make the neat looking structures pictured on the box, which she insisted on buying for our namesakes. I suggested she buy each of them something different, but she was adamant that this toy would teach them to cooperate with each other. I had no brothers or sisters, but I had loads of cousins, and I never remember them being able to get together on anything, least of all Christmas toys. What I saw was the territoriality similar to dogs that mark their territory by squirting urine at points along its perimeter and defending it with tooth and claw. But, she's a school teacher, and when it comes to people under 18, I defer to her greater experience. So, we left the toy store with me carrying a large box under one arm and her clinging to the other.

As we passed the Border's Bookstore, I looked in longingly. I hate shopping, but I love bookstores. I love them mainly because the clerks in bookstores don't follow you around pestering you to get you to buy their overpriced and under-needed goods, instead allowing you to browse the shelves without interference unless you ask for help. She either saw or sensed my look, because she stopped at the large opening and turned to face me.

"You want to go in there and bury yourself in the history section until I finish shopping, don't you?" she asked.

"No, I promised that I'd go shopping with you, and I keep my promises," I said. I didn't even sound convincing to me.

She put a beautifully manicured forefinger against my chest and gazed deeply into my eyes.

"You're not fooling me, hon. I can tell you've been bored out of your skull ever since we got out of the car. I know how much you hate shopping."

"Well, I'm not crazy about it, but I don't like breaking my promises." I wasn't even sure why I'd agreed to come with her. It's not as if she'd stop talking to me if I'd refused.

She raised that beautiful forefinger and tapped the end of my nose.

"You wouldn't be breaking your promise if you enjoyed yourself in the bookstore while I finish my shopping. Technically you'd still be shopping with me. So, you go on in and I'll come back for you when I'm done."

Now, there was my Christmas present.

"Okay, if you're sure."

"I'm absolutely sure," she said. She leaned in and kissed me on the cheek, uncaring that a couple of old biddies loaded down with overfilled shopping bags gave us the evil eye as they passed.

"You know, lady," I said. "That's why I love you. You're always so good to me."

Her eyes misted, and she smiled. God, she was beautiful when she smiled like that.

"You're good to me, too, Al Pennyback, and good *for* me too." She turned to walk away, stopped and turned back, still smiling. "Oh, and I love you too."

I stood there watching as she walked away. I was feeling really good inside. It was going to be a great Christmas.

Charles Ray

# More adventures of Al Pennyback, DC's favorite private eye

### Deadly Vendetta

When a bomb intended for a local mobster kills the wife of one of Al's old army buddies, and the law doesn't seem interested, it's up to Al and his friends to see that justice is done.

### Death Wish

In the wake of the 9/11 terrorist attacks, there is a lot of money to be made in working for the government. There are some who will do anything to earn a profit, despite the best efforts at oversight. When a young sergeant who notices irregularities goes missing, his commander asks Al to find him.

### A Deadly Wind Blows

Al is hired to find a missing heiress and convince her to return to Washington to claim her inheritance. Someone is determined to stop him, even if it means killing him.

### *A Time to Kill, A Time to Die*

A man who spent ten years on death row is finally executed. A day after his death, new evidence comes to light proving his innocence. When the judge who sentenced him to die gets a threatening note, the judge hires Al to find out who sent it. As Al digs into the case, he finds that there's more to it than meets the eye. He finds himself in a race against time against a ruthless killer, who is willing to kill again and again to keep the truth from coming to light.

### *Deadbeat*

Chris Cross is a small time con man. When he runs a con against the relative of a local gangster, he has to flee for his life. His girlfriend asks Al to find him and keep him safe. But, can Al keep himself safe from an angry mobster?

See these and other books by this author at: http://www.amazon.com/Charles-Ray/e/B006WMLEZK

# Other books by this author:

**Al Pennyback mysteries**

*Color Me Dead*
*Memorial to the Dead*
*Deadline*
*Dead, White, and Blue*
*A Good Day to Die*
*The Day the Music Died*
*Die, Sinner*
*Deadly Intentions*
*Death by Design*
*Till Death Do Us Part*
*Deadly Dose*
*Dead Man's Cove*
*Dead Men Don't Answer*
*Deadly Paradise*
*Kiss of Death*
*Death in White Satin*
*Death and Taxis*
*Deadbeat*
*A Deadly Wind Blows*
*Death Wish*
*Deadly Vendetta*
*A Time to Kill, A Time to Die*
*Dead Ringer*

## The Buffalo Soldier series:

*Buffalo Soldier: Trial by Fire*
*Buffalo Soldier: Homecoming*
*Buffalo Soldier: Incident at Cactus Junction*
*Buffalo Soldier: Peacekeepers*
*Buffalo Soldier: Renegade*
*Buffalo Soldier: Escort Duty*
*Buffalo Soldier: Battle at Dead Man's Gulch*
*Buffalo Soldier: Yosemite*
*Buffalo Soldier: Comanchero*
*Buffalo Soldier: Range War*
*Buffalo Soldier: Mob Justice*

## Other fiction

*Angel on His Shoulder*
*She's No Angel*
*Child of the Flame*
*Pip's Revenge*
*Wallace in Underland*
*Further Adventures of Wallace in Underland*
*Dead Letter and Other Tales*
*The White Dragons*
*The Dragon's Lair*
*Dragon Slayer*
*The Last Gunfighters*
*The Culling*
*Frontier Justice: Bass Reeves, Deputy
  U.S. Marshal*
*Angel on His Shoulder-Revised Edition*
*Battle at the Galactic Junkyard*
*Mountain Man*

## Nonfiction

*Things I Learned from My Grandmother About
   Leadership and Life*

*Taking Charge: Effective Leadership for the
   Twenty-first Century*

*Grab the Brass ring*

*African Places: A Photographic Journey
   Through Zimbabwe and southern Africa*

*A Portrait of Africa*

*There's Always a Plan B*

*In the Line of Fire: American Diplomats in
   the Trenches*

*Advice for the Insecure Writer*

*Looking at Life Through My Lens*

## Children's books

*The Yak and the Yeti*

*Samantha and the Bully*

*Molly Learns to Share*

*Where is Teddy?*

*Catie and Mister Hop-Hop*

Charles Ray

# About the Author

**Charles Ray** has been writing fiction since his teens. He won a Sunday school magazine writing contest when he was thirteen, and having his byline on a short story published in a national publication forever hooked him on writing. During his time in the army (1962-1982) he often moonlighted as a newspaper or magazine journalist, and was the editorial cartoonist for the Spring Lake (NC) News, a weekly newspaper, during the 1970s. In addition to his writing, he was an artist/cartoonist and photographer for a number of publications, including Ebony, Eagle and Swan, and Essence, and had a monthly cartoon feature and did several covers for Buffalo, a now-defunct magazine that was dedicated to showcasing the contributions of African-Americans to the country's military history.

After retiring from the army, he joined the U.S. Foreign Service, and served as a diplomat in posts in Asia and Africa until his retirement in 2012. He has worked and traveled throughout the world (Antarctica is the only continent he hasn't visited), and now, as a full time writer, continues to globetrot looking for interesting things to write about, draw, or take pictures of. A native of Texas, he now calls Maryland home.

Author's photo by Denise Ray-Wickersham

www.ingramcontent.com/pod-product-compliance
Lightning Source LLC
Chambersburg PA
CBHW071504170626
46811CB00007B/2729